HOOKED

Bernie Unrau DDS

CalTex Press

PO Box 69014
162 Ave S.W.
Calgary AB T2Y4S0
www.caltexpress.com

Published by Cal Tex Press
#3413 16320 24 St. SW
Calgary AB T2Y5A1
403-246-0523
www.caltexpress.com

ISBN: 978-0-9782937-0-3

Printed by Amazon in San Bernardino, CA, US; Monee, IL, US; Fort Worth, TX, US; Philadelphia, PA, US; Columbia, SC, US; Mississauga, Ontario, CA; Leipzig, DE, EU; Luton, UK, EU; Torino, IT, EU; Narita, Chiba, JP; Wrocław, Poland, EU
https://www.amazon.com/-/e/B081M9Y1J9

HOOKED c1995, c2010

PROLOGUE

Life may throw us a hook, a curve ball. We may rise to the occasion and bask in the blessings bestowed upon us or be overwhelmed by the obstacles and have our ambitions thwarted. The life lines of several souls cross paths in this portrayal of the search for the 'American dream', elusive for some, yet cherished by others. Hotel California symbolizes this quest as stated by Don Henley: "You can check out anytime you like but you can never leave." Cali, an aspiring actress succumbs to some of her vices vanquishing her goals. The compassion of a few including Dr Arthur or Dr Gum may restore her confidence, composure and career? The story touches all of our lives, the triumphs and the tragedies, sometimes too traumatic and best left only in the realm of thought; or in that nether region between dusk and dawn ....the twilight zone.

1. The Big One?

> "There he stands draped in more equipment than a telephone lineman, being outwitted by an organism with a brain no bigger than a bread crumb, and getting licked in the process."
> - Patrick O'Neil

Arthur had raised the bar astronomically. His persistence bordered on the upper pain threshold. His zeal maniacal. Dr Gum's former colleague and fellow student always seemed to have lady luck riding on his side. Arthur's life was truly a bowl of cherries surrounded by the poor souls in his pit crew, his servants, his serfs and pawns. Even in a field which he knew or cared nothing about he miraculously shone once again. Perhaps he was blessed because he truly believed 'Man's real life is happy, because he is ever expecting that it shall be so."(Edgar Allan Poe) The tall fish tale was likely to make the annals of marlin history and most other marine memorabilia in Cabos San Lucas, the playground for the affluent fishermen. Left to frolic to their own devious devices and tactics, many a tall tale had been spun. But this one topped them all.

It was Dr Gum's last chance to perform. Arthur's sheer dumb blind luck, he wondered whether he had ever hoisted anything other than a shot glass in his life. Dr Gum had spent years in preparation for the grand daddy of all angling events, the Bisbee's Sail and Billfish tournament, gradually reeling upward through the ranks. Each stream and small lake a stepping stone to the open ocean challenge. The motion and methodical methods engrained etched into his mind. Every conceivable move and contortion by a worthy oppon-ent studied felt and committed to memory. The extensive armamentarium carried into battle, surely sufficient to surprise the most unwitting specimen. The sophisticated sonar and modern instant satellite imagery to hone in on the most promising places where the enemy hid or lingered oblivious to their ultimate fate. Arthur simply charged, with his usual zeal like a bull in a china shop, headfirst into the fold. Somehow he always kept coming out smelling like a rose. The sweet smell of success. This scenario was no different. As if his 'accident' weren't enough to dampen his spirits, the title 'casting director' was bestowed upon him, perhaps rightly so? His hopes were wrapped up in the huge white plaster cast, like his magic genie. Rubbing it whenever or wherever he pleased, the genie, like his servants, would grant his wish, however ridiculous or foolhardy it may seem. The term was coined shortly after a stunning stage performance which he had no part of whatsoever. He always stole the show anyway. In this fortunate twist of fate Dr Gum had dragged him from the depths of a slowly sinking career and somehow sealed his fate. He felt he was partly to blame for his colleague's cantankerous crooning. The cast became another comical prop. A focal point in which to direct everyone's attention upon him. He coined the term 'casting director' to kill two birds with one stone. One, in his feverish foraging frenzy trying to find the perfect player in his next picture, perhaps a passionate play to find his leading lady. And two as the corked captain, now the envy of the entire Mexican armada as word spread that he had literally single handedly brought in the biggest fish in Baja history. Not only did he capture the fish after a full day at sea, he scared the crew half to death. His drinking binges had brought on bouts of belligerent behavior and bewildering antics well above the norm for the most seasoned stuntman. The fish's final flail perhaps Arthur's finest hour as his cast entangled in the control levers. The captain was thrown overboard due to the erratic course the ship had taken. 'Lady Luck', the name of the fortune hunter's vessel left them spinning out of control in a state of vertigo. Sick to their stomachs with a pseudo Montezuma's revenge, they held onto the resourcefully constructed rod with their very lives. Somehow, they had strapped Arthur into a converted barber shop or early dental surgeon's chair bolted to the deck of the massive cruiser. The chair allowed a full 360 swivel and a panoramic view of the Pacific. It had the usual tilt, not that the lopsided sailor had ever noticed. His cast always created the comical image of a crusty fumbling fiddler crab, roaming the seashore in search of his crabby mate. The custom plaster cast cushioned the unusual accessory. More of an illusive alien antenna or transponder; rather than the rod strapped onto the souvenir slung onto his arm. With a patch over one eye, a hat, and parrot perched on his aching shoulder, a hook may have been a more appropriate fixture. The crew was surprised that the ensuing battle did not send him soaring over their heads to surf the waves being dragged to his death by the monstrous marlin. In the end it was the mighty fish who succumbed to Arthur's innocent idiotic antics. The cruiser spun wildly out of control and proved to be the fish's deadly death spiral. In the process they even reeled in the captain floundering about lost at sea. The purse, perhaps $3 million? Not bad for a day's work. Just the incentive many employees might considerto escape the doldrums of a ho hum drum lifestyle. Millions have been lured by the relaxing leisure time activity, fascinated by the sheer number of spectacular species. Captured to spend their entire lives in a custom clear glass fishy condo or fried up freshly caught in a sizzling buttered up frying pan. At the top of the competitive chain, most are simply caught for the thrill of the chase, the ecstasy of victory or the agony of defeat, the one that got away. The difference, a few inches from the end of the hook, the result up to ten or twenty feet of fish, up to a thousand pounds of pure delight. Arthur was well on his way to claiming the coveted cup today unless an unforeseen turn of fortune and change in the tide were to occur.

"'Treasure Chest'" mused Dr Gum "Who are they kidding? They might as well name her 'hope chest', for all the tears and broken promises we anglers bore boarding this dilapidated boat." Her decks ever empty albeit for the blood sweat and tears poured into each expedition.

"Just a little string of bad luck, doc" suggested Sanchez, the amazed mariner. He had never seen anything like it in all his years along the Baja coast.

"They must've all gone south for the winter! warmer climes" suggested Dr Gum comically. He was still anxiously awaiting the first nibble. "I haven't had first dates this bad. The most slippery fish offered at least a nibble on his ear lobe early on in the adventure.

"Are you sure we're using the right bait?" questioned Dr Gum beginning to tire of initially tempting tequila shooters and tasty corona with a twist of lime.

"Why don't we taunt them with a little taste of human treats?" he said.

"Are you crazy senor?" as he wrestled a full bottle of Corona from the dentist.

"Why not a little strong drink, we've spent most of the morning feeding everything out here" as he eyed the empty buckets of mackerel. "Besides it might confuse them, disorient them, lead them right onto our hooks."

"He has a point, Pedro." Sanchez scratched his head. He was out of ideas and at a loss for words.

"In time they'll acquire a taste and sense of smell for the tasty elixir. Why, in no time they'll leap onto your decks in search of a cool one."

"You've been out in the sun too long!" reasoned Sanchez.

"I think you're right, I feel a little dizzy." Dr Gum slumped prostrate in his chair, victim of the scorching Baja sun beating onto his cranium. His blood was beginning to boil as he awoke moment-arily. "I didn't come here to stroke out nor strike out!" he snapped.

"Si senor. Our luck's bound to change, soon."

"All decked out and no place to throw.... a line, if God is out there, his phone is perpetually off the hook" laughed Dr Gum. The intense sun had finally taken it's toll in a temporary lapse, a sanilocity, or loss of sanity. Why he had booked this trip he'd never know! Other than joining the ranks of the other 'Bondodontists'. Dr Gum was intent on equaling, eventually surpassing his colleagues who had slowly mastered their cosmetic dentistry skills. After all practice makes perfect, right? As long as your adversary steps up to the plate. He saw his dinner dream date vanish before his eyes. Nothing but an empty plate littered with a few scaly bones and garnish. Scraps the local alley cats had tossed his way. His nightmare continued as he imagined a tug on his line. In the day dream the crew yelled at him relentlessly, pleading with him to reel in the big one. Now that's more like it he mused as the mirage materialized. With superman strength he wound up the left handed reel fast forward in a split second. The fish faced Dr Gum with his blood shot eyes then let out a salty belch before expiring on the deck.

"Senor, senor" said Sanchez as he looked Dr Gum squarely in the eye.

"Oh it's you Sanchez, "I had the most delicious dream, we simply brought the marlin up to eye level then stared them to death."

"Muertre!" shouted Sanchez steamin' mad, about to throw his rod into the pacific as a peace offering, a token to treat his guests with a little more respect.He had snatched the casting rod in mid air ere it sailed over the rail. It had slipped through Dr Gum's hands, still sound asleep during the exchange. Shaken, he finally stirred.

"What the…? Where's the fishy? Why don't you boys do a little fish dance. If the magical hat dance is any indication of your competence, I'll nominate you for the Mexican mariachi idol talent hunt."

Sanchez tossed his straw sombrero onto the deck disgustedly. They fired up his ghetto blaster and began to bounce up and down on the slippery deck. The Jarabe Tapatio, the national dance of Mexico. The enchanting Jarabe or elixir, stirred up everyone's spirits. Tapatio was synonymous with Guadalajara, the cultural capital of Mexico. The flirtatious dance usually performed by an inebriated entertainer intoxicated by a woman's love always lured a feisty female. It may be their last hope? In their drunken state they'd resort to just about anything!

"No, it's done like this." Dr Gum fished around the bottom of the bucket. He grabbed 8 slippery tiny morsels, then upended the bucket. "It'll have to do." He tossed the fish in a heap on the aft deck. He began to dance around the pile to the perplexed stares of his amigos.

"It seems to work for the Chinese!" said Dr Gum. "It's supposed to bring peace, prosperity and a good catch."

"Dis gringo is cuckoo" said Pedro as he spun his forefinger around his ear. One of the men grabbed a scaly slippery flounder and slapped Dr Gum across the cheek, like the 'Monty Python's Slapping Fish Dance.' At last he came to his senses. The heat had certainly caused the sanilo-city, or sudden lapse of sanity.

"I'm cooked!" said Dr Gum. "It probably won't work anyway, the dance calls for 9 fish, I only counted eight, unless one of you gringos ate one?" They looked at each other in total confusion, like the Three Stooges.

"We only fish for sport."

"You're kidding me! All those succulent tender snappers, those flavorful filets, mouthwatering mahi-mahi? Your living in angler's paradise. The fiesta is well worth the wait. I've been dreaming of this fishing trip for a lifetime."

"These Americans, you can't live with them, you can't live without 'em." stated Sanchez graciously.

"Alright, the siesta is over, now let's get back to business."

"There must be some sole (soul) food out there,

why don't you pray to your god of fish."

Sanchez looked at Dr Gum rather curiously.

"You may be a fisher of men…"he began.

"Why don't you make me a fisher of fish?" asked Dr Gum. "Do you know that in Hebrew Dagon was the fish god. Augustine, a Christian church father comically combined the first letters from Iosous Chreistos Theou Uuios Soter, Jesus Christ the Son of God, the words spell Ichthus meaning fish."

"It doesn't matter how you slice it, doc, this voyage is damned! There are no fish in the sea. It's beginning to scare me."

"We can't give up hope, we'll mosey along the Baja coastline back to Cabos, see if we can't stir up some trouble."

Up ahead in the distance, Dr Gum saw a shimmering light or reflection dance off the water. The large cabin cruiser kick-ed up a large wake on either side as it rapidly advanced. Dr Gum thought he saw a buoy drop off the starboard side of the boat. In the sweltering heat he wasn't sure of anything.

"Did you see what I just saw?"

"Hard to starboard."

"Aye, aye captain" Two loud blasts boomed from the snout of the advancing vessel, an armada unto itself.

"It's a Godsend, if this doesn't stir up the waters and bring some fish to the surface, I don't know what will" said Sanchez desperately.

The two massive marine going vessels veered to their right to pass within a prescribed distance permitted during the tournament. No boat was to barge into anyone else's perimeter or approach another angler's area of interest.

"I'm going to give it one last shot, it's my last chance to even the score, and settle a long standing dispute with Arthur."

"Best of luck Dr Gum, but you seem to have forgotten one thing."

"What's that?"

"Your bait!"

"Damn it!" my brains are fried, I'll need a holiday just to recover from this grueling ordeal!"

Sanchez lassoed the last of the mackerel onto the steel hook then crossed his heart and said several hail mary's.

"Santa Maria" barked Pedro, you're not here to marry him to the fish, let him get on with the reelin' ritual."

Dr Gum kissed his rod for good measure as they passed 'Divorce Beach'. He unloaded a mile of line. The hook must've caught something as the zinging of the spool suddenly stopped. The tension in the line went taut. At long last!

"I must've caught a big one!"

2: Cali

"Always look at what you have left, not what you have lost"
- Robert Schuller

The small sea otter surfaced. She clung onto the mollusk, one of 300 species that desperately sought to evade it's captor The bivalve's powerful muscle 'clapped' frantically but could not escape. The young girl pried open the shell to reveal the red meat inside, a delicacy prepared as a soup in sashimi or sushi in many of the finer restaurants dotting the southern California coastline. It was of no value. Her object of obsession, a pearl.

Cali had always been a curious child. She was

caught in a clash of two cultures, perhaps creating her rich diversity and uniqueness, like the thousands of species of sea and wildlife of the Channel Islands, America's Galapagos. It was where the cold currents from N. California collided with the warm waters from the Baja. Like her enigmatic origins, she traced her given christened name either to her mother's side, Califia, the mythical island of California, thought to exist in European lore in the 1500's. In 1532, Hernan Cortez sent two ships to the north end of Mexico in search of the 'Island of California'. They vanished without a trace. Califia is believed to lie submerged be-tween Santa Barbara among the channel islands and the mainland. California may have acquired it's name from similar origins. Cali withdrew into her own world often, picturing herself as the Amazonian warrior queen Califia, leading the other inhabitants, only females. Her mother, an aspiring actress, had given her rich ren-ditions of rather daunting tales from a very early age. Her where-abouts was unknown. Some claim she succumbed to alcoholic spirits or the occult, her slip into madness left her a permanent guest of the Hotel

California, the state psychiatric institute in Ventura. Cali would one day find her! Her father on the other hand had come from shady origins in Santiago de Cali, more commonly known as Cali, Colom-bia, the drug capital of the world. His 'export' business included distribution of the white powder, cocaine, in the confines of the mollusk shells. The culinary delights had found their way into the major fashionable circles. The aspiring actors and actresses seeking the 'American dream' in southern California. The trade route trickled down to the wretched world of the totally depen-dent drug addicts and derelicts. He had always told her the 'world was her oyster', that she'd find 'la perla' (the pearl) some day! Wealth and fame would follow. He was certainly convinced of that. Ironically Santiago de Cali is named in honor of St James, one of the apostles and earliest followers of Jesus. Sanctus Jacobue or Sant Iago the great, the holder of the heeled, the supplanter, the son of Zebede and Salome. His emblem was the scallop shell or cockle shell (mollusk). Christians, on their pilgrammages oft wore the shell on their hats or clothes. For some pagans, the shell was a symbol of fertility for young couples. Botticelli's 'Birth of Venus' is nicknamed 'Venus in a half shell'. To Cali it was simply a means off the island, a passport to prosperity. Her parents had abandoned her early as their own tumultuous lives ended in tragedy. They loved her very much but were caught in a world of delusions, drugs and death. As an orphan growing up in Two Harbors, population of about 250, she had not a care in the world. It was a child's paradise. No urban worries, only the endless wonder as she wandered throughout the American Galapagos. The only other town on the island of Santa Catalina, Avalon with a population of about 3500. The tiny sleepy resort community was a sharp contrast to the glitter and glamour of tinsel town only a stone's throw away 10 miles to the east by ferryboat. The 'Isle of the Blessed' as she had discovered from her immersion into the tales of the chivalrous knights of the round table. The Isle of Avalon, where Sir Lancelot had an affair with Guinevere to disrupt the court of King Arthur. Lance-lot, the only son of King Ban and Queen Ullam, had been taken from an early age by the 'Lady of the Lake' to a mysterious kingdom.

An 'isle of maidens' perhaps not so far removed from Califia? Avalon, the final resting place for King Arthur? Mortally wounded in battle, his sword 'Caliburn'(Excalibur) either thrown into the lake or grabbed by the arm of the lady of the lake as she submerged. Such fascinating folklore thought Cali. The romantic errant roving wandering knight in shining armor performing his deeds to capture the heart of a fair maiden. Also portrayed in the novels by writer Garci Rodriguez de Montalvo, Amadis de Gaula, equally as famous, a Spanish Sir Lancelot as her father had often read to her. The perfect escape, here on her own Isle of Avalon. One day she would leave her magic kingdom to enter the real world, equally as enchanting she surmised. She excelled in the only school on the island, K1-12 and would often have the other children spell-bound by her inventive imagination. Her intense orations inevitably would lead her on a quest to become an aspiring actress; but ultimately to unravel the enigma surrounding her parent's shrouded, sordid lives. She'd lead the other children on hiking trips into the hills to disclose many yarns of the days of yore. The famous

Wrigley memorial, a tribute to William Wrigley, the founder of the largest gum manufacturing company in the world lies to the south west of town in the midst of the Botanical Gardens. She'd proclaim that her father were buried there. That he had exported chicle, (literally the 'sticky stuff' gum Nanuatl -Aztec word) from the Manikari chicle the tropical evergreen tree found all over South America. Of course she claimed he made the gum single handedly. Shipping it to all corners of the globe sailing in his ships the Nina, Pinta, and Santa Maria'. Cali, her father's home town was founded in 1536 by Sebastian Belalcazar who had accompanied Colum-bus on his third voyage in 1498. The kids were bedazzled and likened him to Santa Clause or a conquistador. If only they knew the actual contents of her father's crafty corrupt covert conquests. One bigger fish story after another, she always commanded the center of attention, center stage. The beautiful 'Barcelona bomb-shell' part California bleach blonde, an aspiring Shirley Temple? with a trace of temperamental tropical Spanish blood. A truly cross cultural creative carefree child. Cali dove in one last time that afternoon. The cool water churned as she fought the California currents and the giant kelp forests, or like those of Robin Hood of Nottingham. I'd better be careful she worried. Although her antics and underwater tenacity was more like that of the countless sea lions off Pt Bennett on the island of San Miguel, the least inhabited of the eight islands off Santa Barbara. She frolicked among the other species protected in the Channel Island National Marine Sanctuary. She knew she'd one day grow webbed digits due to the lengthier submersions, a mighty Avalon duck or Ama diver. She found several smaller shells along the sea floor and placed them in her makeshift satchel. Nearly four minutes into the dive, she fishtailed, like a seasoned mermaid and rose to the surface. Suddenly a sharp weighted hook-like object spun toward her. The heavy steel line sank. What are they possibly searching for? The leather-back sea turtle? The energetic elusive creature with a metabolic rate 4x that of other reptiles of comparable size. It usually feeds on jelly fish floating off the islands. The male nuzzles up to a receptive female to 'latch on' He often spends too much time under water desperate to seek sex that he drowns! The California Gray Whale found off these waters had been protected since 1846 by the IWC (Inter-national Whaling Commission) The young are born and protected in the shallow lagoons from sharks, before they make the single largest migration of any mammal; a 16,000-22,000 mile trek from Mexico along the California coastline and the Northern States. In 2005 a lone gray whale was spotted around Tokyo Bay. It attracted immense crowds in April, but eventually became caught up in fisher men's nets and drowned, washing up on shore in May.

Before she could react, the steel hook caught the left corner of her mouth and embedded itself in her orbicularis oris muscles. She tried frantically to free herself as it dragged her to the surface.
The pain, a persistent agonizing throb. She'd pass out soon she fretted, scrawny fish bait for the larger predators. The hook continued to rip through her facial flesh leaving a bloody trail. Fortunately her facial artery was not severed. Her screams were contained in the tiny bubbles she expelled. They burst as they reached the surface but did not

convey the perilous position she was in to the passengers of the fishing vessel. Finally she was yanked from the water. Her bloody body covered the deck of the yacht, a sight akin to the slaughter of a prize Great White. The awe stricken anglers presumed her dead. They tried to revive her lifeless body but were unable to. They had to dispose of any evidence they rationalized. This catch would certainly alert the Coast Guard. Their precious cargo could not! As they tossed Cali back into the water in a cold brutal sea burial, she awoke. Her lungs gasped for the oxygen rich atmosphere. The few breaths of air were sufficient to startle her, arouse her from her morose misadventure. She read the insignia on the stern of the boat as she hit the water, 'Dream Weaver' She swam to San Miguel Island as the yacht sped off in the distance. She'd meet her Mexican murderers again one day. Her first objective and immediate concern was to survive! Cali made a salve from various tropical species and compressed the gaping tear in her left cheek. She had lost a lot of blood. Tired, weary and wondering why this would happen to her? Cali found a piece of shiny aluminum, perhaps from another unlucky shipwreck and saw her disfigured facial features. She cried. Why me God? Any hopes of an aspiring film career dashed. The deep ghoulish grotesque gash would leave her scarred for life she fretted. No future, forlorn, no family to care for her, no hope. She felt like an outcast. “I’ll have to fend for myself “ she mumbled to herself in disgust. The shock of also losing her ability to awe audiences was too much.

“God why have you forsaken me?” she cried, heart broken. She climbed the steep canyon and hiked to the top intent on throwing herself off a cliff. In the distance the sheer beauty, the curious caliche, the sand casts of ancient tree trunks and roots startled her. The raw beauty revived her. I have my whole life ahead of me, I can’t throw it away! Think of what could still be? What I may yet accomplish? I can carve out a career somewhere? Even if only as a circus freak she fretted. “I’ll have to reinvent myself. I am a natural born actress” she mused confidently. The strain soon swept her into a deep sleep. Her Prince Charming, her knight in shining armor lurked somewhere in her sub-conscious. Would he arrive in time to save her? Or was she destined to wile away her last few remaining hours on this desolate rock, albeit as colorful as it was with it's rich floral bouquette. The last tribute on a descent into a deep ire-versible sleep.

A tall lanky hiker stumbled across the bloody facially disfigured body. A naturalist intent on studying the 2000+ species on the American Galapagos.

"My God. What happened to you? Who could have done such a thing?" he stated in shock. He raised her tiny torso and carried her down the dangerous path. A group of naturalists rushed to their aid. They relieved the good Samaritan of his load and covered the child in warm blankets like an infant in swaddling. They affixed her to a make-shift stretcher for the 3-4 hour journey back to the mainland. The child stirred midway to Newport. Where am I? on a barge? to the magical Isle of Avalon?

"No, there is no magic here. The surgeons at either UCLA or USC will need to perform a miracle to keep you alive!" he listened intently to her weak voice.

"For a final burial as King Arthur was laid to rest, to eventually awaken?" she continued to mumble in her semi- conscious state of shock.

"What's this about King Arthur?"

"By the look of it, perhaps the assailants were wielding knives or machetes? They certainly did a number on her!"

"Yeah, you could be right."

"They practically tore her face off."

"What? Where am I?" Cali awoke briefly only to relive the horror. An in-tense surge of pain shot through the left side of her face. She stared into the naturalist's eyes pleading to end the pain. He found a few 392's and codeine based pills then gently raised her head. He offered her a few sips from a water bottle stashed in his knap sack.

"Sir Lancelot?"

"They lanced you a lot" said one of the ornitho-logists among the group.

"Huh?" Rather than a shiny steel helmet or an aged suit of armor, this mortal donned a baseball cap with a brown 'bear' strolling on a green patch of grass. He is heading toward a red star, a red stripe lines the bottom of the circular logo.

"A bear?"

"Griz" stated her prince charming percolating with wisdom.

"Griz?"

"The California Grizzly, a symbol of strength" her deep gash might just as well be the product of the powerful paw he feared if he weren't extinct.

"Stars?" she asked.

"Stars?" it was broad daylight.

"The red star on your hat?"

"The five point star is like the lone star of Texas. This is the Golden State, California."

"You're my shining star" she said struggling to articulate the words.

"Thanks miss. Try to relax. You've been through quite an ordeal."

"Ordeal? I remember rising, being raised from the dead? through a liquid medium encompassing me. Then I was able to breath again" she mumbled.

"Maybe she fell overboard?"

"Bitten by a fish?"

"Shark?"

"Naw, those don't look like bite marks."

"Thank God we found her in time."

"She is rather slim pickens for the vultures and buzzards" noted the ornery ornithologist.

"At least there's more of her than two femurs found by Dr Phil Orr on Santa Rosae Island."

"You mean 'Arlington Springs Man'?"

"After 13,000 years, you'd be nothing more than measly dog bones and fish meal!"

3: On One's Own Hook

"Nothing at last is sacred but the integrity of your own mind."
-Ralph Waldo Emerson

A steady dilaudid drip in the I.V. bulb slowly snaked it's way down the transparent life line. It found it's entry point then quickly dissipated throughout the systemic circulation of the child. Cali lay in a sedated state of slumber, oblivious to her outer debilitating deformity.

"I only hope we don't produce another addicted adolescent!" suggested Dr Gum as he scrubbed in with the rest of the team.

"I hear you" stated Dr Chin. "They usually do

it to themselves out there, then we wean them off in here. I'd hate to think we've created a monster."

The team donned their pink surgical gloves.

"Shall we?"

"My God. I don't believe I've seen one this bad before."

"A butcher if you ask me."

"Any leads yet?"

"I don't know?"

The nimble fingers abraded the salty wounds, then applied their craft. They carefully carved away the necrotic tissue, cleaning, cauterizing, contouring either stratified edge of the gaping canyon. They delicately descended into the rift, hooking the ends of the tiny severed arterioles. The main trunk, the facial artery miraculously intact spanned the gap, like the Golden Gate Bridge. Soon the other smaller bridges were teased to span the abyss. The minutes passed. The scrub nurses cleaned the salty beads of sweat from the surgeon's foreheads. Cali did not need another drop of deadly sea water soaking her wounds. Slowly the two fleshy masses were drawn to a close with the thin silk sutures. The rift was repaired with a regenerative kick start.

"I think we've given her a fighting chance!" said Dr Gum.

"Yeah, I think we're good. These sutures will take a knock out punch" said Dr Chin pleased with his performance.

"Knock on wood. She's a knock-out. Once the wounds heal, with those looks she outta be in pictures."

"You have a point."

"We all appreciate a helping hand once in a while."

"Amen brother. I had to claw my way through 'on my own hook'."

"Likewise. Unlike some of the sophisticated preppies who simply displayed their peculiar plumage, then pranced around the med/dent programs. Their tons of cash couldn't buy an ounce of objective orchestrated operative skills."

"They were always off somewhere else. Like their patients didn't matter, merely a means to an enriched end."

"I'm surprised they didn't lose more on the

table."

"I always placed my cards on the table, full disclosure. No hidden strings or agenda."

"What you see is what you get."

"I just hope Cali recovers without any physical scars. The trauma she'll unfortunately carry with her throughout life."

"With guidance and career counseling, she'll make it" said Dr Gum confidently. "Why, I'd hire her myself, show her the ropes, I'll bet she'd make a great assistant. The charts indicated her immediate family is missing or dead."

"She'll probably end up in state run facilities."

"Unless…"

"Are you saying adopt?"

"I've got my hands full" said Dr Chin. Karen's busy with the three little stooges."

"I couldn't begin to commit to a family yet" reasoned Dr Gum. I'm only at the start of my residency. I can't pay my bills as it is. I'll have to hook a steady stream of patients when I get into private practice…"

"She'll make some family very happy."

"Probably a greater capacity for compassion and empathy considering what she's been through."

"Well, I'm off on rounds. No rest for the wicked" stated Dr Chin.

"I'm up to my eyeballs in alligators and charts" snapped Dr Gum.

"I'll check up on her later."

"Ease her off the joy juice slowly."

"I'll do my best!"

"That's all we can ever do."

"I only wish I could take the time off to attend some of those conferences. All those exotic locations, so expensive."

"You need an angle."

"What do you mean?"

"A surgical patent, a product, make your millions. The manufacturer's are always looking for the next big one, idea that is."

"For global distribution?"

"Every clinic, office…"

"And when you do?"

"They'll reel you in, hook line and sinker."

"What do you mean?"

"Perks, profit sharing, mucho pesos my friend."

"I may even pay off a few student loans. Hmm…. I'll give it some serious thought. Thanks Dr Chin."

"Don't mention it."

"No gimmicks though! No peacocks!"

"Peacocks?"

"Superfluous plumage? Show and pomp, glitz."

"You are the brains, they are the brauns… together you can make lots of money."

"Easier said than done."

"You want to be a player don't you?"

"Definitely."

"Then, put on your thinking cap, let your creative juices flow. One big idea, that's all you need. Then you can say you you made it on your own hook!"

Cali was released later that week. Her recovery was a long rocky road, but her wounds healed remarkably well. She was grateful for our gifted work. Her traumatic train wrecked life was on track again. As with the tremendous patient load we lost touch with her…..

Inspired by my intuitive colleague, I embarked on an enterprising endeavor to fill a gap in post graduate studies. My own interest and curiosity in biomaterial science led me on a quest for a polymer to replace tissue lost due to trauma, burns or deterioration due to advanced aging. A complex problem indeed, best left to some of the brighter minds, the true nobel laureates. I steered into uncharted waters. Since nothing natural existed or was years away, why not simulate the natural tissues? I sampled biopolymers from the smoothest polyurethanes used in artificial hearts to prosthetic polymers used in the film industry. Ironically the same labs where 'Flubber' originated. It may not give you the added 'bounce' you are seeking in life or disclose the location of the elusive 'fountain of youth' sought by Ponce de Leon, but it did supplant a niche market for inexpensive 'skin' and periodontal tissues, artificial 'gums' to practice initially suturing techniques. A simple yet sophisticated simulator which any medical or dental student would need to hone their surgical skills. At a fraction of the cost of the manufacturer's models we played with in med/dent school, they soon sold like hot cakes. The perks included an entire arsenal of instruments to replace or arm a practice. The more enticing luring leads on the lecture circuit were the countless cute contours right out of the pages of "Cosmopolitan' or 'Vogue' magazine. I often wondered if Cali ever ventured onto the runways as the years went by? A real 'looker' able to lure any clientele I calculated. Perhaps too shallow a career choice? I was disappointed we lost touch. I did want the best for her as did Dr Chin. He continued to build a thriving reconstructive surgical practice, while I kept a basic dental practice afloat. My passion was in pursuing novel ideas, patents, ways of perfecting surgical techniques with inexpensive alternatives. To train and reach as many residents around the globe as was humanly possible, time permitting. One who gives freely may receive freely as well I found. The more I gave the more I received! The perks kept coming, the conferences were held in ever more exotic locales. I had to find a way to let the lectures pay for themselves. The answer? sponsorship, selecting the most strategic meetings. The ones with the most global exposure. Reach the most number of residents and seasoned clinicians. I wanted to attend a particular conference in Cabos. Soak up some sun, sample the delectable seafood San Lucas is renown for, and catch the big one? A unique giant fish trap, the Sea of Cortez formed after a violent earthquake 10-15 millions years ago along the San Andreas fault. It severed a strip of land 1000 miles long, terminating at Land's end at the tip of the finger at Cabos San Lucas. The nutrient rich waters plunging up to a mile in depth, host over 650 species of fish. Known as the 'Marlin Capital of the World', an annual outing since 1980 became the largest fishing event on the planet. The prize money in the Bisbee's fishing tournament, an unbelievable purse, more than Wimbledon, the Masters Golf, even the Indy 500. Potentially $3 million for the big kahuna, the biggest fish among 153 or more entries. Cabos San Lucas named after the patron Saint Luke, the Syrian of Antioch, the physician by profession. He was a disciple who follow-ed the Lord and Paul. Unfortunately he never took the time out to marry, or have children. He died at the ripe old age of 84. Happy? Perhaps? He followed his heart! He followed the lead of Christ, went about doing good, healed the sick, exorcised demons and spread the word of the Lord. He documented the savior's life, death and resurrection. A peculiar sighting of Jesus after his resurrection was a blessing bestowed upon the local fishermen. (Luke 5: 1-11 KJV) A catch of 153 fish? The number of known species in the Greek world at the time. In fact so many fish were caught, they could barely haul in the heavy nets. If ever I needed a prayer, it was now. Would history conceivably replicate itself? This is one instance I prayed for a miracle repeat performance. Up against the most seasoned professional anglers, I had only a few alternatives. Align myself with a tactful team of trophy winning fishermen or hire the most methodical Mexican marksmen. Their intuitive sense of San Lucan waters as keen as the Academia of San Lucas in Rome. Equally talented artisans who portrayed symbolic icons in religious art. St Luke was considered the 1st 'iconographer', the person portrayed looked like the real person, yet the background was distorted. The color gold represented heaven, red divinity and blue, human life. Perhaps St Luke could bless us with a bountiful catch of big ones? The minimum size set at 300 lbs, excluded many a fine specimen. I thought it best to learn the basics of blue fish sport fishing, then progress to a competitive angler status. Master the rod, the reel the bait, eventually become a master baiter. The essentials of the sport like my career included the competitive edge, the chase, the challenge, the tactics. To out think a tireless oppo-nent. I had to turn a lot of theory into a powerful practical performance. I required the proper armamentarium like my surgical equipment. Hook, rod, bait, reel, line….Ancient hooks were made of bone or wood. Later steel led the way for it's ability to pierce the fish's mouth. Usually barbed galvanized, bronzed or nickel plated leaving a natural color of silver, bronze or matte grey. Today a full rainbow of color's exist, red and black particularly popular. The gauge or gradient of hook depends on the size of the fish's mouth.13 to1, 1/0 to 6/0 in ascending order. The hook is concealed within the bait. Worms, night crawlers, insects and fish are most commonly used. Mackeral is preferred in Cabos waters 75% of the time, sardines also suffice. Electronic and plastic lures have surfaced lately. The hook is attached to the test line and if it can't be removed from the fish's mouth upon capture has to be cut. The early fish lines were silk thread or horse hair with catgut leads. Since 1850 linens and silks were machined or braided and twisted into thick lines. The modern lines are made of artificial substances-nylon, polyethylene, Dacron and Dyneema (UHMWPE), the highest impact strength of the plastics and resistant to corrosive chemicals, odorless, tasteless, non toxic. It has been around since 1979, it is 15 x stronger than steel, thinner than traditional monofilament lines, very little stretch so instant response is felt by the pull of the fish. Flying line is a monofilament wrapped in a waterproof plastic sheath, such as PVC. It may be coated with 'microballoons' or 'air bubbles' or silicon lubricants to enhance buoyancy and prevent wear. The fishing line is wound or spun onto the reel, as acetate film is wound around a movie reel. Comprised of a spool mounted on an axle. Fishing reels first appeared in Chinese paintings about 1195 AD. In America, the bait casting reel was invented by George Snyder from Kentucky in 1820. The bait casting reel or conventional reel in the US. is an overhead mounted revolving reel, made commonly of brass, German silver or hard rubber. A right hand crank to retrieve the line is in use most often, some lefty's have emerged. The larger reels, the 'Big Game Reels' which we'll use in Cabos are for the heavy saltwater species of fish, the marlins, sailfish, tuna and shark. Finally the reel is attached to a rigid rod. Bait casting rods are he stiffest. Up to 7.5 ft long. Able to support the heavier lures and natural bait, there is usually a trigger shaped projection at the end to hook the rod with one's forefinger to steady it. The eyes, for the line, on the rod are small and vary little along the length of the rod. Fishing rods must date back to ancient Egypt, Rome, Greece and China . They had to be light, strong and flexible therefore typically made of split tonkin bamboo, Calcutta reed or ash. The newest rods are carbon and boron composites for greater casting accuracy, distance, and fish fighting abilities. The 'heavy action' rods are less flexible for bigger prey. You are in control, not the fish controlling you! I was now armed hook, line and sinker with the latest data on bringing home the Black and Blue marlin, the yellow fin Tuna, Skipjack, Dorado or more popularly Mahi Mahi, even Jack or Rooster fish. I looked forward to the showdown in San Lucas. I had to check the conference dates, to coincide with the tournament and assem-ble a trusty crew. The challenging catch was there, waiting for the taking, in Cabos.

4: Hotel California

"If life is a waste of time, and time is a
waste of life, than lets get wasted and
have the time of our lives." - Anonymous
"I used to have a drug problem, now I
make enough money."
- David Lee Roth

Dr Arthur Sperry, no relation to the topsider boat shoe empire, had always lived by the motto: "it's your life, don't water it down!" To his closest colleagues, his buddies back in dental school he was simply 'Arthur'. A life of privilege in the posh palm treed neighborhoods of Beverly Hills, Beverly Glen and Bel-Aire, pampered from early childhood.

Attending the finest prep schools and clubs, the world was his 'Rolex oyster'as he comically referred to it. His go kart to greet the new kids on the block, usually had them screaming, scrambling for their lives. The dune buggy to dissuade the sunbathers along Pacific palisades always kicked up a dust storm for the perilous few who frequented the beach. Arthur was a devil-may-care youth. At the riding stables he placed itching powder on the jockey's saddles, until he was caught. He soon indulged in every sordid sorority prank. His remote control helicopters delivered a water bomb full of manure to unsuspecting classmates. The holy terror's imagination continually dreamt up the most devious, diabolical dilemma. His well heeled media mogul father Arthur Sperry the 1st, always got Arthur 'off the hook' with a light reprimand. He felt the child should be free to ramble and roam (RR) Eventually Arthur would reach an age of accountability rationalized Sperry.

"If only you'd channel your energies into viable ventures" pleaded the perplexed professional. "Any one with your temperament would be keel hauled or confined to the corral!" he insisted.

“Perhaps, I’ll give him the reigns, let him produce a film of his own?”

“But father, I have no aspirations to assemble a group of actors, allow them to act out a regimented role.”

“Why not?”

“Anti authoritarianism is ingrained in my soul” he stated defiantly.

“Let them do as they please.”

“But if the right script were to come along? You may have all the wildest stunts you can dream up. It’s what you’re best at isn’t it?”

“I suppose you have a point, father” mulled the bored but brilliant pre-med student. He never seemed to study…the mundane texts, but the beautiful student bodies. He was a natural at assessing each of their conditions, maladies. He read them like an open book. Perhaps a career as a writer would suit you? suggested Sperry.

Arthur vehemently denied. He’d find his own destiny. Live out his dream. Perhaps even bankroll a film about his zany adolescent antics, ‘The Life of King Arthur’ he prognosticated.

“Preposterous!” snapped the elder Sperry, “I’ll

have none of it. It’s sacriligious. You have no respect for anyone let alone a sovereign ruler of the royal realm, such as King Arthur.”

“What do you suggest?”

“I propose you sow your wild oats, first and foremost finish your studies, then if the right script falls into your lap, I will personally bank roll it.”

“What is the right script?” probed Arthur.

“I suggest you study a vast library of them, as you seemed to osmose your medical dental curriculum without cracking a text. You have a gift of visual recollection.”

“I’ll do it!”

“When will I know?”

“When you can pull the sword from the stone” quipped Sperry.

“What does that mean?”

“In other words, when you can extract a story line from a script.”

“Hmmm.” mused Arthur.

“Yes, I will begin my quest for the holy grail, the holy reel so to speak.”

“By jove, now you’ve got it” re-marked Sperry pleased with his son. He may have come to his senses? While most other students struggled to simply survive, secure their grades and the rigorous schedule, Arthur squandered his savings. He indulged in every sordid conceivable sorority stunt yet miraculously maintained his medical school grades. At times he seemed bored. In fact, fuming! He'd develop his own medical curriculum, an educational 'B'movie library to assist underprivileged students, the bring out the 'M' (marvelous) in medical curriculum, the 'D' (dramatic) in dental school courses. He considered himself 'Sir Dean Arthur' the new visionary for nanodentomedicine. There must be an Emmy winning script in there somewhere he mused? Arthur had to find his leading lady, his fair maiden, to lead him through this vast maze of medical mumbo-jumbo. A lurid love story to elucidate the language of medicine. He began an intense interview process. Basically setting up shop in the Beverly Hills Hotel, his 'consulting suite'. Arthur's absence from classes began to worry the profs. Occasionally they'd bring him in for a 'spanish inquisition'.

"Arthur, you attended only one of my classes, yet you received the highest grade, 98%. What do you have to say for yourself?"

"Well professor, had I missed your first class, I'd have scored 100%!" The profs were peeved, perplexed, yet powerless to impede his progress.

The Beverly Hills Hotel is one of the leading Hotels in the world. Built in 1912, it is a central locale to meet people, conduct business, and osmose the austentatious atmosphere. Business was booming. Arthur appeared in his peachy beach print to procure a picture. He became a permanent fixture blending in perfectly into the peachy pink wall paper and ornate adornments. Pink vases contained rosebuds to accent the pink tablecloths.

The offers kept coming.

"I have a simply ducky drama for you dear" stated a statuesque secretary, her gender in question.

"Thank you, Sophie."

Arthur perused through the perfumed parchment entitled 'Harder They Fall'. A proposal for a remake of Humpphrey Bogart's final performance in 1956, some scenes filmed at the Beverly Hills Hotel, the story of Eddie Willis, a broke boxing writer who has lost his sporting column. He is hired by Nick Benko to act as a publicist for Benko's up and coming boxer, Toro Moreno. The fights have been fixed to boost his career. Arthur reflected on his own ascent. How much was due to his own effort as opposed to power and paternalistic privilege?" In the end Benko is convinced Toro is a real boxer, the fight is not fixed!

Arthur, though hardly a physicalperformer prone to violence, saw potential in the film. His own struggle to excel, to please his father, but primarily to find himself, tossed it into the 'think about it' pile.

'The Way We Were' seemed to strike a peculiar chord with Arthur. The 1973 film with Barbara Streisand as the rebellious anti war student is smitten by Robert Redford, a successful screen writer. However, he cannot meet her demanding expectations. She'd rather see him develop his talents as a true literary writer. He savors the affluence and leisure. Streisand (Katie) is pregnant with child. They divorce and meet in NY years later. Redford (Hubbell) is offered a job as a nameless writer with Carol Ann (Lois Chles) a beauty under his arms. Katie remarries, daughter

Rachel by her side. They simply reflect in a brief moment, 'the way we were'.

Arthur is infatuated by the female lead role, her quintessential quest for fame fortune her sky high unattainable standards reminded him of his preposterous parent's pleas. Yet he concurred with the colloquial quote: 'behind every successful man is a strong woman'. He sought a feisty female lead to star in his film.

Arthur's attention turned to 'California Suite', Neil Simon's 1976 bitter sweet star packed comedy. 5 couples are couped up in 1 hotel suite. The first couple is from NY engaged in a bitter custody battle. The 2nd couple from Philadelphia is suffering from an adulteress affair. The 3rd couple from London, she is named for an Academy Award, he is gay. The 4th couple from Chicago is constantly bickering……..Alan Alda, Jane Fonda, Walter Matthau, Bill Cosby, Maggie Smith, Michael Caine, Richard Pryor, etc are among the star studded cast.

"Does it tickle your fancy?" questioned Sophie.

"Too much squabbling! I love it!"

"This one just came my way. It reminds me of...."

"The Bad and the Beautiful.... Not bad!" mused Arthur. "Best actress, best actor, art, set, costume, screenplay. A culturally significant film, inducted into the National Film Registry in 2002, hmm". The lives of a screenwriter, actor and director made it thanks to Shields (Kirk Douglas) but also betrayed by him. Son of a notorious filmmaker, who was shunned by the film industry himself. Shields finally starts a film himself but botches it! The studio dumps Shields, who begs to redeem himself.

"I love it. It's tailor made."

"For who?"

"For me!"

"I do believe you may have a hit."

"Thanks Sophie. But where will you film it?"

"Why right here, several sequences from the original screenplay were shot here."

"Take your time Arthur. I don't know how you do it? You have too many irons in the fire!"

"A mental agenda. A ledger in my own mind."

"Isn't that a legend in your own mind? or time?"

“Thanks Sophie, I don’t know what I’d do without you.”

“Another drink Arthur?”

Arthur’s confabulations continued. Each elixir induced his intoxicating humor and imagination. He fabricated an entire foreign lingo of terms thoroughly confusing all around him. King Arthur and his nerds of the round table as he addressed them with his slobbery slurred sermon.

“Sir, may I remind you, that you are at the Beverly Hills Hotel, not Chucky Cheese” stated the waiter concerned.

“I’m only taking care of business….”

“Good Lord, he’s going into practice?”

“My dear…Peter” stammered Arthur as he stood up and leaned into the name tag of the exceptionally attired waiter. “Practice makes perfect” he said “Peter, you’re approaching me property” said Arthur mimicking ’Yosemite Sam’ directly into Peter’s chest pocket and name tag. Peter eased Arthur into his ‘throne’ amongst the scripts scattered all over the pink pastel booth.

“Perhaps you’d care to take your affairs into the ‘Polo lounge’?”

“Precisely Peter. Peter Piper picked a pack of pickled papers, but how many potential picture scripts did Peter piper pick?”

The world famous Polo Lounge, the perfect backdrop for the budding billionaire film tycoon. Arthur had a vast talent pool at his fingertips, producers, directors at his disposal, beckon call. But in the eyes of his associates, his alcoholic binges impeded any viable venture.

“Arthur, if you can’t clean up your act, I’m afraid we’ll send you to Hotel California.”

Arthur burst into laughter. “But we’re here.”

“Are you sure?”

“Yes, come on, we’re in the Beverly Hills Hotel, It’s on the cover of the Eagles album. One of the top groups of all time. Hotel California!”

“That’s not the Hotel California we had in mind.”

“Well I don’t know what goes on in that dusty little dungeon of your….” snapped Arthur, but I’m not going an where. I’m here!”

“We’re referring to the Camarillo State Hospital…the other Hotel California. You’ll be in good company.”

"The Camilla Steak Pit?" slurred Arthur." But I've eaten, rather exquisitely I might add.".

Camarillo built in 1936 housed thousands of the crazies, loonies, alcoholics, pedophiles, and dangerous offenders. Many were brutally tortured with 'electroshock' therapy. The old administration plagued the hospital until it closed in 1997. Film crews have reported moving objects, coincidental deaths, and unusual encounters. Those who enter the old building are afflicted with headaches, nausea, dizziness and feeling tired. (Keith Richards says he gets ill when he gives up drugs) The laughter of children in the former children's area are common occurrences. A beautiful woman in white, presumably a nurse wanders the halls, but vanishes when confronted. A former employee, a nurse Debbie was shaken violently by a ghostly form while trying to light a cigarette. No one was present. On a film shoot in may 2004, doors slammed, microwaves thrown to the ground, film items missing, only to be found in closed locked rooms. The crew finally quit. It was too terrifying a set. In 2000 a complete makeover began. The former forensic mental hospital buildings were convert -ed to the campus of California State University-Channel Islands. In 2002 CSUCI opened its doors through a grant from ETS (Educational Talent Search) A challenging stimulating environment for deserving scholars to reach their goals and dreams. The ghostly souls have remained to roam the classrooms. The ghost of Marilyn Monroe and Howard Hughes among other celebrities have appeared throughout California.

"Arthur, Arthur" Sophie tried to stir him staring into space.

"You're all crazy! You need to be comforted" he slurred.

"You mean committed?"

"Yes I'm committed to this project If your heart is not in this venture I can let you all go! I am the director here" stated Arthur demanding a little respect.

"Relax!"

"Relax?"

"Relax in Camarillo, Charley Parker of jazz fame composed that tune after his stay in 1947. A little R and R never hurt anyone. MASH was filmed in the hills behind the hospital."

With that statement, the astute alcoholic and aspiring film producer stormed out of the Polo Lounge.

"The only 'Hotel California' he'll film is on the road to nowhere in Todos Mexico, when Sperry Sr takes away his millions" said Sophie sinisterly.

5: Hook Up?

"In the course of history, many more people have died for drink and dope than have died for religion or country."
-Aldous Huxley

Cali awoke in a drunken stupor. She raised herself from the rotten rags and rancid smell to peer out over her confines, a darkened dumpster. She pushed the lid, now sufficiently preheated to fry an order of bacon and eggs. The mid morning rays reached down to comfort her, warm her, perhaps warn her of her impending doom; as she descended further into her delirious states and tremors. She squeezed the last ounce of strength from her ragged, withered form to hoist herself out of the putrid pit. Lost some where in east LA, she wandered as a mad nomad in the desert, or as a refugee in a war torn country. The deserted streets littered with garbage gnawed at her feet. The shredded remnants of her sandals little comfort to her soles. Her 'miraculous' facial surgery a few years back may have left her craving more of the comforting powerful pain medication. Her own miserable painful existence, nothing but a blurry blend of beautiful rainbow highs and eerie hallucinations. All attributable to a gradually growing assortment of pharmacopiea. Her stunning looks had landed her a few bit parts in commercials, but her persistent rebellious nature had resisted the regi-mented regime. She ultimately paid the price; a series of no shows or fashionably late, left her promising career in the crapper. No producer wanted her. The drugs had taken their toll. She had shed her former sun drenched skin. The salty sea breezes of the Channel Islands caress-ed her complexion shaping, sculpting it into a potential future Chanel # 5 cover girl. But that was in a land long ago, far, far away, now as elusive as her enchanting kingdom of Avalon. How she longed for her 'blessed isle'. Instead she wandered this teenage wasteland, nare a Prince Charming in sight. The sun beat on her mercilessly. Her form toppled onto a weedy empty lot. Surprisingly a few hardy wild strawberries had emerged, eking out a small niche, battling the dandelions. Vic-toriously they now enveloped the empty garden. A lush strawberry field flowing forever. A few rose buds burst around the perimeter. It was an earthly paradise, an oasis in the midst of this unruly urban jungle, fit for a princess. What seemed like an eternity passed ere she awoke. A friendly tanned weathered face, that of a migrant Mexican gardener stirred her. He had discovered her while hoeing his prized cash crop.

"Senorita? Are you alright?"

She was startled by the gringo and his decadent sombrero. A few furry balls dangled around it's perimeter. The hypnotizing motion dizzied her. Certainly not the glistening head gear of her Galahad.

"Si?"

"See?" His head gyrated eyeing his blonde sleeping beauty. The sombrero danced up and down, occluding the intense rays intermittently.

Cali bordered on an epileptic seizure brought on by the blinding bursts of light.

"Stop it!" she shouted. "You're driving me crazy."

"Si" he smiled eager to service his sleeping princess. She grabbed him by the chin straps and drew him near.

"If you ever do that again, I'll wrap your balls around your head!" she snapped.

"Si" he said startled by the feisty vixen, the bonita blond.

"But Jose only meant well…..Jose Feliciano."

"Well Jose, can you see by the dawn's early light, I'm one messed up magnolia blossom."

"Mary Jane?"

"No Cali, Cali Columbia."

"No I mean Mary Jane, Marijuana Acapulco Gold? Panama Red? to help you relax! You are one high strung senorita" he said as he released her tight gripping fingertips from his sombrero strap and eased himself slowly off of her.

"Get off me!"

"I just thought you came out to play in my empty garden, bonita?"

The words seemed to magically soothe her. The lyrics of La Isle Bonita began to dance in Cali's head.

> 'Tropical the island breeze
> All of nature wild and free
> This is where I long to be
> La Isle Bonita
> And when the samba played
> The sun would set so high
> Ring through my ears and sting
> my eyes, my Spanish lullaby…..'
> (Madonna, La Isle Bonita lyrics)

Jose, her San Pedro, offered her a tiny rolled cigarette. Too small to be a Cohiba or any of the pricier Cuban cigars her father often lit following one of his successful 'business' or 'fishing trips'. He never took her once, claiming they'd always troll in treacherous waters.

"It's a rare strain. I have cultivated it here. Panama Red. You like?"

Cali greedily grabbed the tiny green roll and inhaled deeply. The drug, genetically related to Columbian Red, raced to her brain resulting in a delicious psychedelic high. It relieved her of her immediate concerns, momentarily. She was grateful to be alive, a taste of a dying culture, and his hospitality. 'Panama Red' died with the advent of cocaine trafficking but the song survived, sung by the lead singer and vocalist Jerry Garcia, during the psychedelic era of the 'Grateful Dead'. A legend who left a legacy of lyrics, Rolling Stone considered him the 13th greatest guitarist of all time. He died of a heart attack due to sleep apnea. Constantly battling tobacco drug addiction, particularly China White Heroin and Cocaine; he was staying at the Serenity Knolls rehab center in Forest Knolls, CA at the time.

The warm smell of colitis rose up through the air. The high wore off quickly. Cali's seasoned consumptive habits sent her into a paranoia inducing state. She felt she'd be entangled in the weeds, strangled by the vines, her vices if she did not get out of there. Jose tried to humor her, console her.

"Don't worry be happy. I have something to show you. See?"

"Si."

He showed her the slits in the stalk of the golden colored plants. "It brings out the flavor and intensity. La manzana de la discordia. (Manzana, spanish- apple or 'city block')

"The golden apple of discord. In Greek mythology, it would go to the goddess, the prettiest, the fairest, fueling a feud between Hera, Athena and Aphrodite a bonfire of the vanities, which eventually led to the Trojan war" stated Cali craftily. Jose offered her a golden reefer of Acapulco Gold or Santa Marta Columbian as two other women wandered into their private 'garden'.

"Ah chiquitas, I'd like you to meet Cali."

"A Columbian connection, Jose?"asked one of the racy raven haired beauties."

"You are always one step ahead of us, that's what I like about you!" Rosie spun him away from her charming competitor. Cali, a rose among thorns. In the thriving green industry in Los Angeles, of some 60 co-operative gardens dotting LA county. She had to stumble into a seedy illicit operation. The $171 million dollar industry provides much needed employment for the low income immigrants and indigenous population. The program, unique to California, trains new gardeners and aspiring horticulturalists. It also supplies a rich variety of fresh fruits and vegetables to supplement their diets. A pride of owning one's own garden and self sufficiency shines through. The UCCE (University of California Cooperative Extension) program provides for food banks, shelters for abused women and the homeless, halfway houses, and seniors.

It was time to leave, Cali felt she had outlived her welcome. Two's company, three's a crowd .she struggled to regain her composure, but her head swirled, her synaptic cravings satiated by the soothing scents. She ran from the three amigos desperate to deputize the desperado. In the confusion she slammed into an LAPD cruiser patrolling the shady neighborhood. She bounced off the door leaving a pronounced dent in it. Her head hit the pavement. The last thing she remmembered was a giant star emblazoned on the door which impacted her. The shock combined with the streaming sunlight sent her into a petit mal seizure.

The officer called for an EMS dispatch then climbed out of the cruiser. Her dilated blank pupils stared vacantly into space. Hopefully no brainstem injury had occurred. He found no ID, nothing amongst her rags.

"This is where I long to be, La Isla Bonita" she repeated over and over like a broken record or in a trance.

The stunned Mexicans sank to their knees. "Sanctus, dominos." They prayed to God, yet claimed she was possessed by a demon spirit.

Cali awoke in a room cuffed to a bed. The stark bare walls, certainly not the Hilton.

"Welcome to Camarillo, miss."

"Camarillo?"

"Hotel California, Camarillo mental hospital, what have you."

"We had you hooked up to the banana bag for a day. Your blood alcohol was about .4, we thought you were dead. Most anyone else your size would be. The other toxins in your blood had us very worried. Traces of cannibis…" stated the other attending in his bleached white lab coat.

"Why am I here?"

"You posed a threat to everyone, particularly to yourself."

"A threat?" I'm no threat, I'm a movie star!"

"Sure Shirley Temple, that's what they all say! Most of our guests get back on the saddle and jump start their shaky careers, but they're usually well established. You're so young!"

"Others are not so…."

"Lucky? Like my mother!"

"Your mother?"

"Christina Columbia."

"Christina?" He scratched his head. "I'll have to check the records."

"You've had some terrible night-mares and hallucinations."

"What?"

"Sometimes you're clawing your covers, like your trying to flee for your life escape from something or someone." The physician guessed she was a victim of severe child abuse, but Cali could not or would not remember.

"You keep repeating 'This blessed Isle, of Avalon.."

"We'll have to keep you here. It's for your own good, until you clean up your act, then 'you can check out anytime you like, but you can never leave!'" (Hotel California, 1st track from album by the same title, lyrics Don Henley) stated the institute's attendant with an eerily insane smirk on his face. Wasting away in the wretched rehab resort, tending to the terminally incurable, had taken his soul.

It sent a chill up Cali's spine. The sooner she'd be free, the better. She heard the staff mumble a few more words as they left.

"Nobody saves America by sniffing cocaine, jiggling your knees blankeyed in the rain, when it snows in your nose, you catch cold in your brain." (Allen Ginsberg, poet 1926-1997, the year of closure of Camarillo)

"Today's kids can put dope in their veins, or hope in their brains. If they can conceive it and believe it they can achieve it. They must know it's not their aptitude but their attitude which determines their altitude." (Jesse Jackson)

"Did you come up with that?"

"No, I think it was a famous movie star who spoke those memorable lines. I think I've been hanging around these re-covering actors too long!"

It stirred her, inspired her. Cali had to fight back, win her life back.

She awoke from her own haunting nightmares often to the screams of fellow psychiatric patients.

Heavily sedated by psychotropics or neuroleptic medications. She had often refused the phenol-thiazines Chlorpromazine and Thorazine used to treat thought disorders and hallucinations. She feared she'd end up like one of the young patients. K.C. had experienced hallucinations, mosquitos on his bed. He refused the drugs. He was later given a neuroleptic, Haldol. Neuroleptics can cause extra-pyramidal symptoms such as tremors, akathesia or general discomfort and restlessness, difficulty swallowing and involuntary protrusion of the tongue. Also involuntary movements or dyskinesia as well as breathing problems. A counteractive anticholinergic, Cogentin, may cause toxic brain syndromes and vomiting. K.C died of cardiac arrest shortly after administration of the drug. The other victim J.V. died of asphyxiation of his own vomit locked in his room. He had actually died in the washroom but the staff had moved the body to the bed where other staff members thought nothing of it, thinking he'd merely sleep it off.

She had to get out before she'd succumb to the same hideous fate, at the hands and fingertips of fumbling fools. Administrative apes who failed to follow protocol eager to 'enrich' the patients with all manner of prescribed potions.

"Witchcraft!" she fumed. "I have to escape. I'll decide the manner of my own poisoning" she laughed facetiously. Her soul had sunk to the very depths of hell she thought. Things could not conceivably get any worse. If these other struggling dregs, actors and actresses could drag themselves from the depths of despair and addiction, then I'd follow in their footsteps. The experience left her with renewed hope. She heard gentle whispers from within the room before she fell asleep that night. Perhaps encouraging words from her mother, her enduring spirit was always with her.

The very next day, she simply walked off the cultivated haute coutured grounds, never once looking back. It was now a page from her past, used only as kindling to her fiery imagination and indefatigable restless spirit. Her mother would have done the same, had she survived? Cali hadn't a clue to confirm her death. She'd continue her quest, kick start her career somehow. Follow in her imaginary legendary footsteps like Marilyn Monroe or a host of other Hollywood starlets who literally rose from rags to riches by their own sandal straps. She removed hers and tiptoed to the edge of the road. Cali reflected briefly over her 'hospitable' stay at the 'Hotel California'.

"Such a lovely place, such a lovely face" she said adjusting her bangs in the broken motorcycle mirror she found by the side of the road.

6: Lucky in the Sky with Diamonds

"Why is there all this controversy about drug testing. I know guys who would test any drug they came up with."
- George Carlin

Cali gave the thumbs down to Camarillo then raised it to hopefully hook the first passing motorist. The scenic seaside stretch of highway snaked along the pacific. The first few cars zipped by thinking she might be a crazed patient from the nearby facility Cali presumed. The shadows lengthened into the afternoon. Her feet were tiring, treading on the pebbles. She thought it best to head to the beach, let the sand sooth her soles. A siesta or even snooze perhaps bed down for the night. The silence was suddenly interrupted. In the distance, a rumbling grew, the occasional loud blast, gunfire? The roar intensified. Not a cloud in the sky she thought. A silvery black silhouette approached rapidly. A Harley? A hog? Cali had longed for a ride as long as she could recall. The shimmering shiny spoked showpiece stopped only inches from her toes. Two heavy black boots stamped the pavement. The black leather chap leggings ended at the waist. A red white and blue American flag draped the upper torso of the muscular motorcyclist.

Cali was confused. She didn't know whether to salute or scramble for her life down the steep incline to the seaside.

"Captain America?" questioned Cali curiously, staring at a splitting image of the character from 'Easy Rider'.

"I get that all the time" said the biker in a cross between baritone and tenor voice.

"I'm Zeke."

The geek or freak thought Cali.

"I suppose your zeeking America?" she blurted out without giving it any thought and began to giggle. Zeke's scarred face and demeanor changed to one of ire and wrath, then burst into laughter.

"I haven't found it yet, but perhaps you can help me look Princess? By the way what's your name?"

"Cali. I, I don't know" she said Cali cautiously. 'Would I accept a ride from death?' she deliberated as she studied his features carefully.

"Listen sister, you're one raggedy Anne. All dolled up and no place to go. I'll take you away from here. You've come from the 'Hotel, Cali'? am I right?"

"Is it that obvious?"

"You have check out written all over your pretty little face."

"Well Andy I suppose…"

"Hop on." He handed her a rotund racing helmet emblazoned with an American flag as she crawled on the hog behind him.

"Thanks, it's beautiful" she hoisted it over her head and fastened the strap. He revved the horses, then left a cloud of smoke as the two desperados roared down the highway.... the dynamic duo, destination unknown.

Cali clutched his midriff and hung on for dear life unaccustomed to this racy form of transportation. Her methods, more modest, limited to biped-al motion. The constant vibration and rumbling were playing congas on her kidneys.

"I have to pee, can you pull over please?"

Zeke zipped to the side of the road. The motorcycle lurched to a stop. Cali dashed down the grassy embankment and squatted behind a few small bushes.

"Thanks. Can we take a brake? A pit stop?" She yelled as she peered to the distant dunes tapering down to the sandy stretch of beach.

"Sure."

He hauled his heavy frame and hog off the road down a beaten path. He booted the kickstand and balanced the bike on the soft surface. It shimmered in the sunset reflecting a golden radiance. Cali curled up near the warm engine and stared off into space. Zeke eased himself onto the cool sand and lay back propped up on his elbows eyeing the sheer emptiness.

"Can I offer you anything?" asked Cali rather boldly. "I mean a reefer, Panama Red?"

"Don't mind if I do. Can I lace it up a little?"

"Huh?" Cali was thoroughly confused, his boots had no laces.

Zeke saturate the rolls. It absorbed the solution like blotter paper.

"Just a little something to ease my weary bones."

"LSD?" said Cali perceptively. Her knowledge of many pharmacopoeia had grown phenomenally. Not the text book kind; the street smart study of samples. She was ready for more tasting.

"As long as you're OK with it?" "I'm glad you asked, unlike the 'room service at the hotel' where they ram it down your throat if you resist. There were two deaths recently."

"Reminds me of some of the medical experiments the Army was into years ago."

"Oh?"

"Yeah I had a brother who served in special OPs on various secret projects. He knew some of the biochemists who were working on various biological weapons experiments."

"You mean drugs?"

"Yeah, particularly LSD, mescaline, even a 'truth' drug. In these cases, however, the drugs were administered unwittingly."

"How do you know, they didn't know?"

"Project MKUltra and MKSearch"

"A MC What?"

"No, not the Mc BLT, hold the cheese kind! I'm talking CIA, FBI, covert operations. Have you ever heard of the Church Committee?"

"Church?" Cali had never even set foot in one. "You mean the buildings with the crosses on top everywhere?"

"Sort of, this Church was fighting for the rights of the common folk."

"Like Captain America?"

"I suppose."

"Anyway, this committee led by senator Frank Church began to probe the illegality of CIA and FBI activities. Ted Kennedy revealed what they had uncovered in 1977."

Cali was feeling a strange sensation, the LSD was expanding her mind, her heightened senses, awareness, she sought to hear more. She eyed Zeke, his form took on an aura, a trail of pixilated or geometric images as her eyes darted back and forth. Perhaps she was slipping into pleasant slumber or synesthesia? But his words came out melodically, making her feel at ease. Cali was ready for a magical carpet ride.

"I'm all ears Zeke!" The words seemed to form as they left her mouth.

"Project MKUltra was led by Dr Gottlieb, who descended into some dark diabolical methods. Patients were submerged into sensory deprivation chambers while unknowingly administered with LSD. He even injected himself and wrote down the results."

"I should keep a diary of my experiences" suggested Cali.

"It gets better. The deputy director of the CIA was later implicated in 30 universities who had extensively tested and experimented on unwitting citizens. Americans from all walks of life, social class, foreigners."

"Extracurricular projects?"

"No, they weren't part of any core curriculum. These were completely clandestine cover ups."

"How did they and you find out?"

"As I mentioned, my brother was a biochemist with the biological weapons research division. There was one mysterious death, initially ruled a suicide. Dr Frank Olson. Who was part of the top secret OPs at Ft Derrick in Frederick, Maryland. He was opposed to biological weapons."

"So they silenced him?"

"So to speak. He was given LSD unbeknownst to him. He developed severe paranoia and a nervous breakdown."

"I feel fine" said Cali lapping up the lecture. The words seemed to flow from her lips.

"The CIA transferred him to New York to see one of 'their' psychiatrists."

"And?"

"On his last day at the mental institute, Nov 28, 1953, he leaped from the 13th floor to his death."

"Leapin' lizards" shuddered Cali. A tiny gecko lizard crawled up her leg. Zeke quickly swatted it. It was no hallucination."

"So it was a suicide?"

"His son Eric Olson always felt it was murder. The autopsy determined by Prof Frank Starrs of Georgetown University, cause of death blunt force trauma" (The incident in the film Good Shephard) A long drawn out case finally got to the bottom of it. The Army had tried unsuccessfully to hide medical records to save their hides. The CIA exported MKUltra to Dr Ewen Cameron in Canada, who was paid $69,000 for continuing experiments. In addition to LSD he used electro-shock 30-40x normal power. Lawsuits were pending."

"What goes around comes around" agreed Cali.

"Amen, sister. How are you feeling? No adverse effects?"

"I'm feelin' fine. Flying high."

"Just keep me posted. I'd hate to see anything happen to you."

"Thank you Captain America, that's the most considerate thing anyone has ever said to me lately. The truth always seems to come out."

"In spite of the cover ups, the CIA certainly thought so. In 1964, the MCSearch Project was in the midst of perfecting a 'truth' drug for former Soviet spies."

Cali likened Zeke to a super agent or spy. The 'Spy who loved me' or 'Spies like us' as her fertile imagination wove a vivid fantasy. Perhaps the legend, Zorro, fending for the rights of the poor and oppressed?

"Another strange incident occurred prior to Dr. O's death. Harold Blauer, a healthy, fit as a fiddle, tennis player voluntarily admitted himself into the N.Y. State Psychiatric Institute in Dec 1952. He was feeling depressed due to his recent divorce. On five different occasions he was injected with three different mescaline derivatives. The drugs were administered under false pretences by US Army Chemical Corps to determine the effects of Chemical warfare agents. After the first, he felt ill from an adverse reaction. He informed the nurses during the first four injections. They said he'd be returned to Bellevue. The 5th agent was 16 X the previous dosage. His body stiffened, his teeth clenched, then began to foam at the mouth for two hours before lapsing into a coma and died. The medical records were removed by the US Army, critical evidence in a mal practice suit. The mother and daughter received some compensation only after a lengthy series of trials."

"Why the cover up?"

"The Yanks wanted to keep up with foreign governments if you ask me. After all American prisoners were being tortured with mind probing techniques in Korean prisons during the Korean war. They were tough nuts to crack!"

"But to go about it under such cover…"

"It's been with us since the beginning of time, the powerful and influential program their serfs into sub-mission. The people are merely pawns in their games. No guts, no glory, just greed!"

"I feel life has tossed me a lemon inspite of society's attempt to squeeze me into a specific role to play a particular part."

"Now you're talkin'" stated Zeke "keep the creative juices flowing!"

"It must be the LSD speaking, the syn…?

"The synesthesia, the semisyn-thetic psychedelic has that power over people. Depending upon your state of mind, experiences. You had a small dose."

"I like it, I feel I can fly." Cali stood up dizzily as if in slow motion. She twirled around like a pretty ballerina. The panorama around her barely kept up with her, frame by frame of special effects. The dazzling golden sunset, a series of geometric patterns gyrated around her out of sync

Zeke caught her as she neared the water's edge. He had no intention of let-ting this nubile nymph drown.

"Do you remember the movie 'Easy Rider'?"

"Do I? It's the 88th best film of all time, slated for the National Film Registry. Best Actor, best writing, story, screenplay It was the director's first film award."

"Remember when Wyatt Earp and Billy the Kid pick up Luke, from the commune? Who offers them the LSD."

"Sure."

"Prior to my imprisonment at the hotel, I had passed out in this field of strawberries which flowed forever."

"An LA co-op commune?"

"Later George, Jack Nicholson, the ACLU (American Civil Liberties Union Lawyer) bails out the jailbirds, for 'parading without a permit'! George joins the posse."

"To look for America?"

"Mardi Gras, and the brothel George suggested. They each meet a prostitute, not that I'm implying anything miss."

"No harm done."

"But it isn't until they venture into the cemetery that…"

"That what?"

"That they experience a wild trip on LSD."

"What happens to them?" Zeke hung his head, nearly in tears. "The bikers are killed by red-necks!"

"That's horrible." Cali hugged the large lovable lummox. "There, there, it's just a movie."

"Yeah, but in the back of my mind, that could be me!" The LSD had stirred a sensitive chord in his collective memory.

"One day I'll ride my harley up to the pearly gates without a parking permit."

"That's ridiculous!" laughed Cali "there's always room for one more hog in heaven" she snorted uncontrollably.

Zeke was so happy of being informed of this he reached into his inner vest pocket and pulled out a small bag of shiny cuts stones. "Here, they're yours."

"But I couldn't."

"Simply a token of my appreciation."

"What are they?"

"Diamonds. You won't have to worry about anyone controlling your life again." The diamonds sparkled in her eyes. The excitement was too much for her; She dozed off in his arms.

They awoke early, stirred by the crashing surf. The cool breeze rushing through her hair on the back of his harley was as close to heaven she could imagine. He dropped her off an interstate in east LA.

7: Questa

"Enjoy the stream oh harmless fish
And when an angler for his dish,
Through gluttony's vile sin
Attempts the wretch to pull thee out
God give thee strength gentle trout
To pull the rascal in!"
-John Wolcot

The cool crisp morning air aroused the eager anglers as they stepped onto the dock with the last of their gear. The coolers packed to the brim with 'Budweiser'; once depleted, ample space to store the assortment of Kokanee, lake trout, bull trout, whitefish, and west slope cutthroat. Fit for a fiery evening cook out and festive celebration, our knives and forks were sharpened. Hank, 'the hooker', our faithful guide, intended to live up to his reputation of making fishermen out of all of us. His motto: 'Give a man a fish, he'll eat for a day, teach a man to fish and he'll sit in a boat and drink beer all day.' He set the bait casting rods delicately at the stern of 'The Flathead Flounder', a misleading title bequeathed on the aging vessel. Out-fitted with the latest underwater sonar, she'd hauled in many an unwary foe. The feisty fresh water fish usually lurked in the deeper waters. Hank, the chivalrous alchemist had perfected the appropriate formula for catching trophy size fish. I handed him the tackle box containing a vast collection of lures. Such exotic names of flies- elk hair, gold dare-devils, lead A gators. We'd always win with a Zimmer's country mile lure, he boasted. His recipe for reeling them in, watch for the tug on the line, wait for the tug of war, then wear them out! The rest of the essentials were already on board, life vests, sun visors for the intense fall rays. Topped up with fuel prepared for a long leisurely cruise on the vast expanse of water.

"The Flathead Flounder left the peaceful dock

at Marina Cay. Nestled in the sheltered sleepy bay at Big Fork, one of the top small towns in the US founded back in 1901. It's 1400 inhabitants, a rich blend of business folk, 50 specialty shop owners and artisans. 13 art galleries, crafts and trinkets. The best theater performance in the NW, the Big Fork Summer Playhouse.

We cast off and set out on our adventure. The vessel veered to the right of a mighty pillar, a gate, a 'fork in the road'. Outbound traffic to the right or starboard, inbound to the left, port. The bridge, split the northern 1,000,000 acres of the gorgeous Glacier International Peace Park from the south; endless acres of pristine forest, rolling hills and plains.

We'd certainly outperformed the outfitters of our predecessors. Lewis and Clark in their early expeditions weighted down with only the essentials in food, furs for clothing, warmth and shelter and a trusty canoe. Out to explore the vast un-charted region to the west of the Mission Mts. The shore-line receded as we entered one of the largest inland lakes in the western US, Flathead, one of the clean-est fresh water lakes in the world. Across the vast calm glassy smooth surface, the Salish Mts. Named after themselves, 'the people' the native American Indian tribes extending from the Bitterroot River to the Snake River. The tribe pleaded for the 'black robe' missionaries to preach the gospel to them after encountering Lewis and Clark. Instead, under president Buchanan, an expedition led by the future president James Garfield was sent to oust the tribes. The 'Treaty of Hellgate' in 1855 tricked the natives by translation issues into leaving their homeland. The gold rush of 1864 created further tensions. In1871, they had forged the signature of the former chief's son Chief Charlot, 'claw of little grizzly', for his reluctance in ceding the land to the US. The Bitterroot Salish, Pend O'reille and Kootenai relinquished over 22,000,000 millions acres unbeknownst to them. In the process they were pushed onto the Flathead Reserve.

"I suppose you've all heard of the Lochness sea monster?" asked Hank as he eased the vessel midway into the 30 x15 mile body of water.

"Just a legend!" quipped Dr Gum.

"Well, be that it may, we had our own Flathead monster to contend with. Caught by my father, God rest his soul."

"No, that's just a fish story!" snapped Dr Gum.

"Early one morn, reckon' darn near to the day back in 1955 he set out to tackle the terrible beast. That very day after a fierce tug of war, he wore out the venison of the deep. You see most of the big fish rest near the bottom of the lake for most of the year. Only in September do they come up to the surface. Why, at that time you can practically yank them out in less than 10' of water in the shallow bays."

"No kidding? Then what are we doing way out here."

"The fresh air'll do you good."

"It is turning into a spectacular day, I'll admit."

"Besides, I want you to learn to cast your lines without hooking any of the neighboring boats let alone anglers on our own vessel."

"You have a point there, Hank."

"Getting back to my fish tale, It was this very spot, near the deepest point on the lake, He reeled in a really big one, 181 pounder, Whitefish."

"Please!"

"Stuffed, sitting in the Polson –Flathead National Historical Museum as we speak."

"Of all the liars, the fisherman is the most trustworthy"(William Sherwood Fox, Silken Lines and Silver Hooks, 1954) stated Dr Gum skeptically.

"Reading about baseball is a lot more interesting than reading about chess, but you have to wonder, do any of these guys go fishing?" (Dave Shiflett, Houston Chronicle 1990)

"Al right, I'm ready!" Dr Gum whipped his hook line and sinker into the water. A small splash disturbed the mirror smooth sheen. In less than a few seconds, he felt some resistance. He toyed with the line, teasing, tempting his lake trout. The slippery foe fought furiously for a few minutes before Dr Gum had retracted most of the line and flung him onto the deck.

"She's a beauty!" he yelled. The fish flapped and slapped on the slippery wet surface. Hank slid toward the twenty pounder and thumped it once on the head.

"There's more where that came from" said Hank proudly holding up his prize.

"I've only just begun" said Dr Gum surprised by his 'beginner's luck'

Hank cracked a Bud and tossed it to the'fisher-man'. Dr Gum caught the can ere it flew over-board.

"Nice catch!"

"Thanks, you may try a little slow pitch some-day, that's baseball."

They whiled away the hours.

"Before you know it, I'll make 'fishaholics' out of you yet" said Hank as they slowly made their way back to the bay. Dr Gum spotted a limp sail in the distance ahead. A whisper of a breeze was all it took to inflate the large main sail of the sleek vessel which hugged the surface. It shot forward across the bow of the cruiser.

"Did you see that?" asked Dr Gum "as if fired from a sling shot."

"Those older Q class yachts were something else weren't they?" marveled Hank.

"They're so sleek."

"The pride of 'Herreshoff', one of the leading designers of yachts for the America's Cup races out of Mystic seaport. The sail practically pulls her through the water on a wisp of air. The narrow beam only about 8', propels the 51 footer like a rocket."

"What is she called?" asked Dr Gum.

"Questa, Spanish for search." built out of Alaskan cedar in 1929 by JP Morgan, only about 13 or so remain restored. By the time she was built the regulations for the race changed. Most boats were in the 23 m range."

"What a shame!"

"Why? rather than in the company of the ultra rich, she is in good hands."

"How so?"

"The ranch hands of the Montana Dude ranch restored her. Doug Averill and the boys bought up most of the land you see right over there, 2000 acres. The Montana Dude Ranch ranks in the top 2% of resort destinations in the US."

"Well you've whet my appetite, in fact, I'm hooked! I'll slowly work my way up to the big leagues" said Dr Gum.

"Glad to hear it" said Hank as we passed under the starboard 'gate' into Big Fork Bay. "Mighty good eatin' this evenin' I reckon" he stated excitedly.

The precious memories and practice, left me craving for more. I proceeded to continue my quest in preparation of the Bisbee's Tournament. Progress to bigger boats, more open waters out on the ocean. Talented crews to teach me the ropes, the ins and outs of trophy fishing. I looked forward to my next outing.

We passed under the wide gap, sufficient to swallow up the Spanish Armada; it's lofty arches high above us allowed the likes of multistoried Nimitz class nuclear powered aircraft carriers to cruise on through. San Diego, home to both the largest naval fleet in the world and one of the largest yacht clubs in America, the host of the 1995 America's Cup race. We were but a mid sized fishing yacht 'Smoothie' set out for a three hour tour off Pt. Loma.

"The Old Point Loma lighthouse is part of the Cabrillo historic monument named after Jose Rodriguez Cabrillo, a Portuguese sailer, sailing for Spain, and the first European to navigate San Diego harbor. One of the prime tuna grounds" We targeted our sights on taking home thick fileted slices for sautéing. "In 1602 Sebastian Vizcaino arrived aboard the 'San Diego' from New Spain, naming the area after the Spanish Saint, Didacus (more commonly San Diego). Following the end of the Mexican – American war and surge of the gold rush of 1848, the city became the seat of power for San Diego incorporated in 1850. It grew into the larg-est collection of naval facilities in the world and reputedly the 'birth of naval aviation'. It was the setting for the 1986 film 'Top Gun' based upon the real TOP-GUN program at the Naval Air Station Miramar. The 'bar' scene of the Kansas City BBQ is on the corner of Kettner Blvd and West Harbor Dr. near the Grand Hyatt. After the defense and aerospace industries decline, the economy diversi-fied. Qualcomm headquartered here, and a major player in biotechnology. Genentech, ranked one of the best 100 companies has numerous medical patents including Activase, a clot buster, Nutropin a potent growth hormone Tarceva, for colon cancer, and countless others."

"Where are all the other yachts coming from?" questioned Dr Gum.

"You mean the bottleneck up ahead?" yelled

captain Connor.

"Yes."

"Well you better get used to it, the traffic will be equally as heavy out of Cabos San Lucas harbor during the upcoming Bisbee's Tournament. This is but a taste."

"If they're all out here after the same thing, Genentech will have to begin cloning gills, scales, fins, the complete package to replenish these waters."

"Nah, there's plenty for all out here, one of the prime tuna spots on the west coast." He slammed the steering wheel.

"Of course, I should have known." The harbor master alerted the small craft of the last leg of the race off Pt Loma.

"Race?"

"The finals of the coveted 'America Cup' yacht race!"

"How many contenders?"

"Just two left?"

"A duel to the death?"

"You might say that. Between 'Black Magic' from New Zealand out of the RNZYC, skippered by Russell Coutes and defender Dennis Connor aboard 'Young America'. (who eventually lost 5-0)"

"Any relation?"

"I get that all the time, but no!"

"Important?"

"It's the 'Holy Grail' of yachting. The ewer, or bottomless pitcher, made from Britannia silver, it's the oldest, most coveted trophy in international sport, predating the Olympics and FA Cup. The longest running stretch in the history of sport, 132 years, belongs to us Yanks."

"That's quite a stretch!"

"It aligns the best boat designers, builders, fundraisers and team efforts to try to take the prize. The first boat to take the cup, 'America' of course. The earliest competitions were held off Long Island, the NYYC from 1853-57. The winning designs by Nathaniel Herreshoff from 1893-1920. (US) A stiff contender, the Scottish tea tycoon, Sir Thomas Lipton lost aboard 'Shamrock from 1899-1930 aboard the very large 36m (120') sloops. The races were held off Newport Rhode Island from 1930-1983."

"I sailed aboard a Q Class racing yacht the past few summers…"

"The Questa, one of 16 grand old girls left. After WWII the J class yachts were replaced by the 12m class yachts. (65'-75'). The unthinkable occurred in 1983."

"What pray tell?"

"Bond. That's what happened."

"007?"

"No Alan, from the Royal Perth YC aboard Australia II. The 132 American year reign had come to an end."

"Son of a ..gun."

"The top gun for awhile!"

"In 2003 'Alinghi' the Swiss entry defeated Larry Ellison's BMW Oracle racing out of San Francisco's GGYC (Golden Gate Yacht Club) 4-1.

"When's the next big one?"

"The 2007 America's Cup is slated off the coast of Spain, between June 23 and July 7th. The 1st time it will be held in Europe in 150 years."

"Larry Ellison as well as a host of challengers will be back for the coveted cup; Alinghi of Switzerland, Emirates team New Zealand, a United

Internet team from Germany and Desafio Espanol 2007"

"What will we do in the mean time?" stated Dr Gum. He was under the gun to hone his hooking skills.

"There's a lot of ocean out there. Considering the earth is ¾ water and only ¼ land, I'm surprised people don't spend 3 X as much time fishing as we do tending to our lawns." Captain Connors cranked the wheel hard to port to circumnavigate the crowds and head for open water.

8: Route 66

"If you ever plan to motor west
Travel my way, the highway
that's the best,
Get your kicks on Route 66"
-Bobby Troup

Cali gave the thumbs down to LA then raised it once more to lure and hook the next passing motorist. A sparkling bag of hope, her permanent passport out of this prison of broken promises and shattered dreams. She ended up on an unmarked stretch of two lane dirt road deviating from the main interstate. It wasn't found on any road map. Yet the historic route traversed state and time in a memorable meandering maze from Chicago to Los Angeles. Cali caught a lift as the last rays of light cracked through the California skyline. She'd resort to resting in the wooded lands on the side of the road if she had to. Her last chance came, fortunately in the form of a Ford, the 1949 town and country classic woody convertible. The nerdy computer programmer pulled over reluctantly and offered her a lift. How appropriate, a trip down memory lane, 'Beauty and the geek' thought Cali to herself with the top down.

"I'm Patrick" stated the scholar "from Princeton."

"I'm Cali, from California pleased to meet you."

"I'm enroute to Chicago on Route 66" he stated boldly.

"Out to get your kicks?" she asked assuming he'd remember the old lyrics and to estimate which era he was from.

"Excuse me?"

"Just kidding, I was just testing you to see if you'd recall."

"I have a perfect 4 point GPA if you're referring to tests" he boasted proudly.

"I'm impressed" she said trying to strike up a conversation. She did not want to divulge much about her shady street smarts to him. He'd likely pee himself in his tacky plaid pants.

"You can be my navigator if you like" offered Patrick as he pulled out his travel planner and assorted maps from the glove box. "I'm taking the original route."

"Go for it Professor P."

"But in the dark, we might miss a turn off."

"Don't worry we'll take our time" she said soothingly. Her soft voice had a strange seductive quality about it surmised the scholar.

"We're on the stretch from Barstow to Needles, on the old National Trails Highway."

"I'll say, it's quite a weather beat-en path!"

"There should be a railroad pass up ahead, if we're on track ha, ha" he blurted out. Cali thought his humor half baked if not downright dumb. "Where's that confounded bridge?" he stated from be-hind his bulbous spectacles. His night vision had a lot to be desired.

"OK Einstein, we're on the I-40 There it is!" shouted Cali excitedly.

"Good, to the south or us is the former Red Rock bridge. It's the original 1947-66 access to California. The bridge was replaced in 1945 with the bridge you see right here."

"Where to Waldo?" wondered Cali.

"Huh?"

"Nothing, I thought of where's Waldo, but we're doing fine."

"We'll wind on down to the Old Trail Arch bridge, which carried the 1926-1947 road."

"Right on. You're quite the pilot Patrick."

"Gee, thanks, but you're the most beautiful co-pilot I've ever seen."

"I bet you say that to all the girls."

"No, I've never actually had a co-p…."

"Watch out!" cautioned Cali. The car nearly ran off the road as it ascended an abandoned area. "We've hit a dead end. We'll have to turn back!"

"No, we can make it!"

"But it looks risky!"

"Nothing this old woody can't penetrate. Watch me! The maps indicate only a sandy wash."

Cali curled up next to Patrick, gripping his arm. Her squeamishness strengthened his confidence.

He gunned the accelerator and spun a gattling gun's worth of gravel off the back balding tires.

"Patrick!" Cali was curiously aroused by his antics. The car lurched forward finally gripping the real road.

"You're such a stud muffin" she teased.

"A stuffed muffler?"

"A chivalrous car driver. Baby you can drive my car anytime" she cooed as she pursed her lips like Marilyn Monroe. The fuel gauge wandered into the red zone. Patrick pondered how long they'd be running on empty.

"Perfect" proclaimed Cali as her acute vision spotted the sign up ahead in the middle of the road. '66 Motel', the former El Rancho Motel sign, now simply a greeting to 'Needles'.

"We'll stop here" suggested Patrick.

"Oh my, but you are brave. I hardly.." Cali's mind wandered.

"Last gas stop in miles. Nothing but desert from here on in."

"You're wearing the pants, you're the boss."

Patrick pulled into the gas station and uncapped the line to the fuel tank.

A strange black van materialized in the distance as a mirage out of nowhere from the desert. The peculiar pentagrams painted on the side, and the '666' plates had Patrick unnerved. The nozzle began to shake in his hand.

"Relax Patrick, there's nothing to worry about, it's just a customized shag-gin' wagon."

The side door flung wide open. In-side an odd sight, an organ amongst the other ornate furnishings. The 'organist' stepped out, draped in a dark black leather suit. A member of Black Sabbath? mused Cali.

"Yeah Patrick, relax" insisted the sinister, dark character as he approached the scholar, shaking, his knees knocking. The figure faced Patrick point blank then tore the spectacles from his face. He threw them to the ground and stomped on them.

"Why did you do that?" asked the astounded ascot adorned lad.

"Patrick!"

"Quiet Patty!" Two beastly band members grabbed the girl and threw her in the vampirish van.

"How'll you get your kicks now Patrick?" asked

the obnoxious ominous figure as he opened the car door. Patrick dropped the nozzle on the pavement in shock. The fuel gushed all over the ground. As the van screamed out of the gas station, a smoldering cigar was flicked out of the passenger's side window. The bright blazing trail of fuel lit up the night sky. As the van roared down route 66, the sign '66 motel' tilted as the flames engulfed it. A fireball sailed into the air as it consumed the car stop.

"Ha, ha, ha" laughed the five passengers hideously as the plumes of smoke appeared in the rear view mirror. Cali was petrified. Her life had taken another deadly detour. She placed her face in her hands and wept. The mascara smudged her high cheek bones, in a macabre mess, as she seemingly morphed into the image of the maniacal band members.

"Great, we could use a new high priestess" stated the satanic lead singer.

"Priestess?" Cali had heard princess, but this term was foreign to her.

"Yes, together we will make beautiful music together. Chants for the 'Church of Satan'."

"Church?" Cali was confused. She had associated church with an organization to do good., as Zeke had explained. Where was her Zorro when she needed him most? What was this, a cult?

She peered around the peculiarly appointed vehicle. A few 'black lights' gave it an eerie glow. The organ; perhaps they were mad musicians? She spotted a copy of a 'satanic bible'. Were they miss-ionaries? She was not sure what to think. You've certainly wandered way off course this time Cali" she thought disgusted with herself. They spoke in tongues, or strange sentences as they introduced themselves.

"We are descendants of the order of the trap-ezoid, the governing body of the 'Church of Satan'. We are following in our leader's footsteps, Anton LeVay, the founder."

"And he wrote this book?" spec-ulated Cali astutely.

"Yes, in 1969 he created the church doctrine. His words of wisdom inspire us." More like created monsters mused Cali. She felt she had to play her tarot cards right or she'd likely end up a sacrificial lamb at the slaughter in this surreal

666 setting.

"You didn't have to kill Patrick."

"Part of the plan. "

"Plan? Premeditated murder?"

"He was taking our high priestess from her true calling. To inspire the next stanzas in the Satanic lyrics and verse."

She felt slightly relieved at her highly esteemed role in this garish game of mistaken identity. I'm damned if I do, damned if I don't, determined to escape this devil's cauldron. The perplexing pentagrams and eerie emblems perfused her mind. The warm smell of colitis fumigated the fancy black leather interior. She found herself drifting off into a nightmarish fantasyland once again. A netherland of lunacy. It was a toss up between the crazy care givers of Camarillo and this diabolical delivery of deadly drugs. The van drove off into the night heading back to the cursed civic cauldron she was determined to escape.

"You can check out anytime you like, but you can never leave" they warned her. She was certainly a prisoner here of her own device. Danger always seemed to knock on her door. The grim reaper never far behind. Perhaps a curse from daddy Diablo, the devil's dealer. She was entrenched in his web of drug warfare no matter where she went. Was this her ultimate fate? forever destined to play out these pentagonous plays. Was this the only role planned for her? A bellicose beastly backdrop of 'B' movie sets from which she'd begin her career? Certainly there must be a brighter future beckoning somewhere over the horizon, her weary soul surmised. The night riders rolled into town near midnight, the witching hour. Cali, a vital part of this vampirish venue, vanquished from the vibrant mainstream.Now dabbling in the dark, nether lands of the night. Anton LeVay had come to California, to play his organ in the burlesque clubs, carnivals, circuses, and roadhouses, even dating Marilyn Monroe, it has been speculated. The organ, actually a calliope, creating sounds by steam through whistles, later known as the 'train whistle'. It began using musical rolls like the player piano. During the 1990 'Burning Man' festival, a pyrophone was used, actually an internal combustion source for the music. It was known as 'satan's pyrophone'. The charismatic leader of the 'Church of Satan' reeled in many distinguished members. He was described as the 'black pope' performing his satanic baptisms, rituals. He died of pulmonary edema in 1997, the year of the closure of Camarillo. A satanic funeral was performed, the body was whisked off to Colma, California north of San Francisco which had banned cemetaries in it's city limits in 1900. Many cemeteries cover Colma. Wyatt Earp is buried in Hill Eternity; Joe Di Maggio once married to Marilyn Monroe lies in Holy Cross cemetary. Abigail Folger, the coffee heiress murdered by Manson lies in Colma. A.P. Giannini the founder of the Bank of America rests there. As does William Randolph Hearst, America's first media mogul lies in Cyprus Lawn Cemetary Colma.

Cali would have to claw her way out of this chilling choreographed chapter in her crazy semi comatose life. The van rode through the less respectable alleys of a seedy strip club district near the outskirts of downtown. The van pulled into a loading dock of the 'Devil's Dancers'. An equally eerie set of back stage hands helped unload the stacks of ‘satanic bibles’, black and bloody red brochures,

“Careful with the organ!” as the cauldron’s crew raised the instrument of their satanic choir. They gave her a choice to audition in the sinister strip joint or die.

She leapt from the unloaded van and dashed down the dark alley. Several black bouncers swooped to surround her. She checked her pockets dejectedly, her bag of diamonds had disappeared.

“The devil’s in the details” she screamed.

“That’s what we like to hear. We’ll let you speak to the man himself” as they escorted her through the darkened cavernous pit. They left her in make-up with a coven of other wenches wrapped in their garish attire.

“Relax honey, it’s the best money you’ll ever make” said the aging burlesque queen. “I’ve strutted my stuff in some of the finest clubs in San Fran, the Condor was one of them!”

“The Condor?” asked Cali unaccustomed to the terms. “A vulturous voluptuous vixen?”

“That’s one way to put it my pretty.” The aging sagging granny reminded Cali of the wicked witch of the west, or worse, on the menu to be stuffed for dinner. Obviously her overdosed episodes were entering her conscious.

"Here, try these on" suggested a shapely buxom beauty, somewhere mid-range in age between the virginal bombshell and Vampirella's great grandmother.

The proprietor from perdition pranced into their premises, waving his bag of diamonds, a payment to prolong his pretty private dancer's sentence.

"Let's see what you've got" said the lecherous lizard, his tongue leaping from his orifice.

Cali slipped out of her rags and forced herself into the tight red leather leggings. She cringed at the snake writhing around her legs.

"Relax sweat heart, just part of the act!" The forked tail dangled between the legs of her jump suit. She pulled her horned hood over her head.

"I'm the devil's daughter!" she cried, examining her red costume carefully in the lipstick smeared vanity mirror. The bright white bulbs seemed to stun her, multiplying in multiple images in slow motion. I must have been drugged again she stated. Perhaps it's just a bad dream?

She closed her eyes for a few moments. Cali concentrated, trying to stay awake during her her 'audition'.

"Just be yourself, you'll do fine! Pretend you're performing for your boy-friend! Show 'em your sleazier side!"

Cali imagined pulling it off for Patrick then burst into tears.

"Come on now, it's this or back to the streets sister" stated satan's advocate.

"Time to shake your booty!"

Cali felt her way through the darkened cavern. She found herself in the center of the steamy smoky set. Plastic multicolored flames danced all around her. The breeze from the fans provided some relief from the heat and perspiration of the clammy costume. The heat was on. She had to turn up the heat, here in this hellish nightmare. The lost souls leered at her, longing for more. An eternity passed ere she found the zipper to her red jumpsuit. The rest of her riveting performance, in tune to the bellowing organ, but a blur. The days turned into weeks and months, then years. Her endless days were spent sleeping while she danced the nights away then stalked the insatiable sad souls wandering the streets in their intoxicated states. She applied her craft cunningly amassing a small fortune over the years. The precocious pupa was blossoming into a beautiful buxom butterfly. Soon it was time for her to leave the larva in the land of the living dead. Time to fight for her life and freedom once again

9. Behind the 8 Ball

"Those who are not looking for happiness are the most likely to find it because those who are searching forget that the surest way to be happy is to seek happiness for others."
- Martin Luther King Jr

Cali sat in a corner booth in the deserted dated diner, something out of 'Happy Days' era trying to remember where the time had gone. She'd heard that 'time flies when you're having fun', but her Ripley's believe it on not existence, was but a blur. She toyed with her caeser salad, spinning the green leaves with her fork. Miraculously she had maintained her stunning looks and figure. All attributable to that very first leaf of coca. The subtle tingling on her tongue tantalized her taste buds. The numbing effect seemed to match the rest of her muted memories. The 'devil's daughters' had encouraged her to consume the anti depressant, if only for a temporary euphoric sense of happiness. Sure it had it's medicinal qualities as a topical anaesthetic in ENT (Ear, Nose Throat surgery) but her main concern was to lose weight, maintain her model-like stripper's shapely form. It was the perfect appetite suppressant. Not only did it curb her craving for the calorie rich cuisine she could finally now afford it, it unfortunately left her physiologically and psychologically hooked. She waved the waitress at the counter and ordered another Coca-cola. The secret ingredient 7 X, the highly contested miniscule amounts of coke, or cocaine. She thought of her father in a favorable form. After all he was supplying the main refreshment supplement in the world. Coca-Cola imported 115 tons of coca leaves from Peru each year, and 105 tons from Bolivia. The US DEA has registries of the import which Coca Cola vehemently denies. How they used it was a mystery to Cali. Perhaps obtain the 'essence' of the leaves through an elaborate extraction process. Yet it cannot be detected even at the molecular level. No matter.

"Here you are miss" said the waitress as she left the tall cool bubbly brown glass on the table.

"Straws?" asked Cali.

"What, are you blind or something, miss?"

"No, why do you ask?"

"They're right over there in the dispenser."

"Oh right, must be suffering from a sun stroke or something."

The waitress shook her head thinking to herself, these Hollywood stars are all the same, they only come in here wearing off a hangover, or about to get high.

As soon as she slammed the swinging door and stepped into the back to take a break Cali grabbed a handful and jammed them into her purse. Next, she poured the contents of a pouch onto her empty plate. With her knife and fork, she arranged a few rows of the white powder as if cutting her salad leaves not to alarm the waitress. Rather than using one of the long red and white straws, she rolled up a hundred dollar bill and quickly snorted her 'caesar salad'. An effective method of procuring a peak effect in a mere 14.6 minutes. Insufflation via hollowed out pens, but since she had not penned so much as a postcard in the past decade, either the straws or rolled banknotes would suffice. Besides, she knew the waitress wouldn't mind the tip. Cali unrolled the bill and brushed off thetable. She accidently tipped the sugar dispenser to cover her tracks, then left without a trace.

"Miss, miss, you're bill!" screamed the wily waitress as she stormed out of the back. She picked up the curled note and cursed "those damn Hollywood high rollers, God bless them one and all."

Cali cruised along the boulevard with renewed vim and vigor, as her ancestors the Arhuacos, the native American Chibcha family of N. Columbia might have. The 'bola' or balls of coca were placed in their cheeks while chewing. The leaves were carried in a woven pouch or chuspa mixed with a small amount of uipta, or lime. The potent mixture allev-iated sleepiness, hunger, headaches, even altitude sickness at higher altitudes. Living in the 'navel of the earth', the Sierra Mts of Santa Marta. The simple subsistence farmers were profoundly spiritual, worshipping the creator 'Kaka Seranku'. Their universal law, the Kunsamu, is passed onto a young Mamo, or village boy, who may continue to train to absorb the culture, medicine and philosophy of the elders. In the early 1900's the Arhuacos sought the spiritual lessons and to learn to read and write. Instead the government sent friars who rounded up the people and herded them into orphanages. Many were forced into slave labor. Cali was determined not to be anyone's slave or servant ever again. In 1943 the missionaries and ministry of Agriculture acquired most of their prime land, later building a TV tower on their sacred Mt. Alguicil. An armed militia terrorized the tribes. In 1975, marijuana crops were introduced attracting many peasants, later forced recruitment created much resentment and violence. The advent of commercial coca plantations created a cash crop for the para military and guerrillas. The Archuacos were caught in the cross fire as the army accused them of counter-insurgency. Many were assassinated as the guerillas gained control of the area. Her father escaped and formed his own farming coop, but was forced to move further inland into the jungle, toward hell's kitchens near Leticia. Here he began to create a cocaine empire, cooking up the highly coveted recipe which infiltrated the counterculture of American society at first. In the 60's, the Beatles Jini Hendrix, Bob Marley and Jefferson Airplane participated in the spreading of the mind expanding exper-iences through the enchanting melodies. Even Sir Conan Doyle dabbled in the delicious dreamy drug. Cali felt she'd assimilated into the American way of life at last. Life in the fast lane, her mind raced on, savoring the transient sensation. She star-ed skyward, and slammed into a stranger on the street. His head struck her square in the jaw, nearly dislocating it. Cali fell backward. Before she hit the star studded walk of fame, a few outstretch-ed arms caught her. Equally as wired as she was, the band members, introduced themselves as the 'Buddy Happy' and the 'Travelling Walnuts'. It needed a little fine tuning felt Cali but at least she was in good company.

A cut above the crazy cocaine snorting 'Church

of Satan'. The only sermons she savored were shortcuts to a new high. There were no short cuts to heaven she came to believe.

"Thanks guys, I'd be seeing stars if you hadn't happened along."

They studied this curious wired woman and soon burst into laughter. Cali couldn't resist and roared out load herself.

"Which way you goin' miss?"

"Wherever the wind blows me" she expelled rather philosophically. "I'm a free bird, goin' to California...."

"She's perfect, birds of a feather...you know" teased one of the tycoons. "Flock together like a flock of eagles" she quipped, she made no sense at all. "Aw flock off" she fumed, her mind bombarded by flashbacks from the black satanists.

"Don't worry be happy!" said one of the African acoustic associates. They sensed she was coming down off her short sensational high. She was probably hooked.

"Can we buy you a drink?"

"A cheap shot? Not this Chiquita! I'll need more of a pick me upper. A penthouse suite and a saddle bag full of pure coke" she insisted.

They couldn't place her face, yet she had a certain star-like quality about her. A seasoned professional or a high priced call girl they presumed. They decided to play along.

"All right, we're all here for a good time…"

"Not a long time" she snapped completing the sentence at the speed of light. She had experienced many close encounters of the worst kind. Her life on many an occasion hung by a tenuous thread. The test line miraculously held so far!

"I'm game" she conceded. "Where to boys?"

"Walk this way!" Cali cruised in her chique high heels and short leather mini skirt which clung tightly to her cheeks, and followed the pack of wolves.

"Hop in sister" they said as they approached a long pink Cadillac parked at the side of the curb, a set of Texas long-horns fixed atop the front grill.

"Bull…" she began. "Be frank with me, Are you boys the 'Blues Brothers' or ZZ Top or …?"

"We're anyone you want us to be" they said lured by the lovely Marilyn Monroe look alike. They fired up the pink panther and headed to a cluster of cabins or bungalows, Chateau Marmont on the Sunset Strip. Cali soaked up the sun as her golden locks billowed in the warm Santa Ana scirocco breeze.

They hauled a black medical bag into the room.

"You're not Dr Detroit are you?"

"No, but we're going to give you a few tips."

"Tips?" Thousand dollar bills danced in her head.

"You're hooked aren't you?"

"I'm not a hooker!" she said, "I gave that nasty habit up ages ago."

"No, hooked!" You have a trail of white powder stretched right across your face from the corner of your luscious lips, snow white!" stated the astute attending with the black bag.

"Please, do you have a mirror?"

"Sure, princess!" The words, she had longed for so long. It stirred her deeply. Her fairy tale may yet have a happy ending.

"See?"

"Si" she said stunned. "I'm a slut!"

"No you're just a little messed up. We can clean you up. You know cocaine is a powerful stimulant?"

"Tell me. A real rush!"

"Your heart's racing, am I right?"

"Yes."

"It wears off quick doesn't it? You wish the feeling would last forever?"

"You know it!"

"Well there's a technique called 'piggybacking'. It dates back to the 1930's." She conjured up all sorts of acrobatic antics. Were these guys circus performers or the three little pigs? She prognosticated.

"Of C and H…."

"The sugar company?"

"No sugar, cocaine and heroin. The two ingredients are mixed or cooked then injected. It's called a 'speedball'. It allows you to enjoy the rush, the Cocaine high, the Heroin has a mellowing effect. It eases you gently from the sudden low."

"No strings?"

"Swear, cross my heart."

"Besides, it's highly fashionable. Many famous people prefer this soothing exciting elixir."

"I want to be in vogue" she said valiantly.

"Don't want to be left behind. Keep up with the Joneses…"

"Jolly Good!" Cali braced herself for the big bang. The solution was prepared. The syringe's thin gauge needle pierced the protruding vein in her forearm. The contents surged up her arm. A heart warming glow engulfed her as the solution shot to her synaptic endings.

"I'm a shooting star!' she stated in a stupor.

"You're a speed demon. Welcome to the C and H Club. You're in select company. Eric Show, the keyboardist of the Grateful Dead. Comedian Chris Farley River Phoenix, John Belushi, Jim Morrison?"

"Stars…..Wait a minute" she worried. They were all shooting stars, whose lights burned out well before their time. Their brilliance faded far too soon."

"She's bright" they ceded.

"How are you feeling?"

"Fine, fellas."

"Yes Robin Williams and Robert DeNero were with John the night he died. Each addressing their own demons at the height of their addiction."

"It's so sad" she cried.

"Don't worry be happy, Cali. As John's tombstone reads, 'I may be gone, but rock and roll lives on!'"

"How very right you are!" She reminisced the renowned performers lives. After all she was still alive. Through all the crazy mayhem in her turbulent twenties. She was still very much a part of the human race. No crash landing yet.

"Come on let's grab a bite"coaxed the consortium of culinary cocaine connoisseurs.

"Sure, my treat" she offered. They crammed into the Cadillac. It rushed down the Sunset Strip into the suburbs. They spotted a popular haunt, a local pool hall and pizzeria.

Cali led the rat pack into the premises. She plunked down a few bills.

"Hey lady, you plannin' to buy the joint?" said the short Italian waiter.

"The boys want to shoot a couple of rounds. They're shining stars you know. A round for everyone, in fact, drinks all around." She felt on top of the world for the moment on this mysterious merry-go-round. Where and when it would ever stop God only knew. For now she was alive, that was all that mattered.

"Sure thing."

"How about some of that fabulous deep dish California pizza for everyone?"

"That's amore" stated the chef as he blew her a friendly kiss.

She was a seasoned snooker player having frequented the numerous pool halls in the precinct. Many a shark and hustler had succumbed to her sweet deceptive charms and cuing skills. She always blew on their balls for good luck. Perhaps an adaptation from the Vegas term, blowin' on some other guy's dice for good luck.

She racked up her balls. Then tore up the table. Ere the aromatic crusty dish arrived at their table, she had downed all but two including the eight ball. She lined up the target but was momentarily distract-ed. In the corner of the room, a curious crooner, hunched over his Budweiser beer. A collection of cute college type co-eds circled the circumference of the table. She was smitten as she miss struck the eight ball. It soared over the table, sailing over the confused patron's scalp.

“Are you alright, Dr Arthur?”

“Now that’s what I call ‘Lady Luck’“ laughed Dr Arthur as he picked up the 8 ball. “Someone seems to have dropped one of their balls” he slurred.

“Let’s get out of this shooting gallery” snapped one of the stunned sorority sisters sparing no time in escorting the inebriated crooner out of the corner. They hustled him out of the pool hall in a rush.

Cali was intrigued. He was an unusual ornament amongst all the other permanent fixtures in the pool hall pizzeria.

10: Some Like it Hot!

"Searching is half the fun, life is more manageable when thought of as a scavenger hunt than a surprise party."
- Jimmy Buffet

Dr Arthur arranged another audition, in the austentatious surroundings he was more accustomed too. The sordid sorority hangouts were simply too much of a shock for his silver spoon life style. His silver screen ambitions were deliberated from another trendy locale. The luxurious landmark, the Del Coronado Hotel. A grand vision which grew in the 1800's. Jacob Gruendike of the 1st National of San Diego had acquired all of Coronado and North Island in San Diego for about $110,000. A 24 page project was planned, entitled simply 'Coronado Beach'. With a few other wealthy investors including Elisha Babcock, railroad baron from Evansville, Indiana and Hampton Story of the Story and Clark Piano Co. of Chicago they began the beach makeover. Completed in less than one year in 1888 for $1,000,000, a pretty penny at the time. It was the oldest and largest all wooden building in California. Designed primarily for the rich and famous, it naturally drew many noted dignitaries through it's doors over the years. FDR, (Franklin Delano Roosevelt), Dwight D. Eisen-hower, John F. Kennedy. Lyndon B. Johnson, Jimmy Carter, Richard Nixon, Gerald Ford, Ron-ald Reagan, Bill Clinton, both George Bush Sr and Jr. It was a veritable venue of presidential royalty. Edward VIII was courting his future wife, Wallis Simpson, residing there at the time. Thanks to Thomas Alva Edison, the bright lights first illuminated Southern California, later with the camera and action. Charles Lyndbergh has taxied through it's corridors, on foot. The Del was credited by publisher Rand McNally as savoring 'more fame and historical significance than any other Hotel in North America'. Thus, it ultimately was declared a National Historic Landmark in 1977.

Dr Arthur was banking on it's prestige and power packing punch to reel in a really big star studded shoe. The beautiful pristine beach an idyllic setting for a romantic interlude such as a remake of 'Holiday' with Cary Grant, the 2nd greatest male leading man, so named by the AFI-(American Film Institute) and his leading lady Katherine Hepburn, the #1 female star of the 'Greatest American Screen Legends', a match made in heaven. The 1938 remake of the 1930 film about a clash between a wayward free spirited playboy's sordid lifestyle, and his ultra rich fiancee's family. Perhaps he'd kill two birds with one stone and find his future wife? A wealthy Californian socialite. It was after all America's number one wedding destination.

"It's a brilliant idea Arthur" insisted Sophie, his trusted confident for most of the aspiring film producer's chapters of his life. He had to get this product-ion off the ground. To follow in his father's footsteps, inherit the family fortune and acquire a little fame of his own. There was one slight catch, a curious condition in the clause. Sophie constantly reminded him of it. A formidable hook; he had to make the film in the United States. No if's, ands or buts. Sperry Sr insisted that American talent was to be utilized exclusively. He could shoot anywhere in America, even an icy epic in Alaska or steamy tropical charmer in Hawaii, or Puerto Rico, but that's where Sperry drew the line. It seemed like such a simple request…

"I think I've found a truly precious gem" gleamed Sophie as she clapped her hands. A tuxedo clad waiter carried the jewel on the satin pillow. He leaned to his highness. Arthur looked a little leery, already lingering in the lush liquors. He picked up the sizzling script and dropped it onto the dark hand rubbed wood desk assembled in the 'Crown Room'.

"Hmmm" mulled the 'movie mogul'.

A silence befell the attendants and staff, as they held their breaths. Several seconds elapsed ere the 'Earl of Entertainment' emitted a response.

"Some Like It Hot" stated the mini mogul from his large throne. His royal subjects let out a sigh of relief.

"Yes, some of us do."

"Shall I turn up the heat, sir?"

"Excuse me?" asked Arthur. "I prefer the air conditioning actually."

"Well?" said Sophie with baited breath.

"Some Like it Hot."

The staff looked at each other rather perplexed.

"The title is terrific! What's it about?"

"Oh, some like it hot" The staff finally understood. Arthur always seemed to bamboozle them.

"I thought it would be right up your alley Arthur."

"How so?"

"In 2000, it was only ranked the 'Funniest Film of All Time'!"

"Really?"

"Really!" insisted Sophie. The 1959 comedy stars, Tony Curtis, Jack Lemmon, and your dream girl Marilyn Monroe."

"Do tell me more."

"Two struggling musicians, Jerry and Joe after seeing the slayings of the St Valentine's Day

Massacre in Chicago in 1929, scram. Spats Colombo, the mobster orders their execution. The only out of town gig they can find is with an all girl's band. They call themselves Josephine and Daphne."

"How devious."

"Wait, it gets better. They both fall for 'Sugar' Kane Kowallzyk, (Marilyn Monroe), the band's lead singer and ukelele player, and fight for her affection."

"I am amused" stated Arthur relishing a steamy romance.

"In a beach resort, actually filmed here at the Del, Joe (Tony Curtis) seduces Sugar by deceiving her claiming to be the heir of 'Shell Oil' in Cary Grant's voice. They ultimately escape aboard a yacht out in Glorietta Harbor here, where it was filmed."

"Fantastic."

"You think so?"

"Sophie you're a genius" as he reached up and gave her a slobbery salty kiss, nearly tipping over his tall strawberry marguerita.

"Why thank you Arthur " she said enamored as she wiped the wet signature of his affection.

"There were a few memorable lines from the film, which by the way won Best Costume, Black and White. Marilyn won the Golden Globe for Best Actress,while Jack won Best Actor. It is ranked the # 1 comedy by the AFI (American Film Institute) and #14 of the 100 best films."

"Say no more."

"But don't you want to hear the lines?"

"Surprise me Sophie."

"It's the story of my life, I always get the fuzzy end of the lollipop… real diamonds, they must be worth their weight in gold! Last but not least, 'the ship is in ship-shape shape'!" cooed Sugar (Sophie) "Oh I nearly forgot,
Jerry: Have I got things to tell you
Joe: What happened?
Jerry: I'm engaged
Joe: Who's the lucky girl?
Jerry: I am!"

"Yes, I do declare we have a winner! But wait where will we find our leading lady?" inquired Arthur. Sophieleft completely deflated, dashing any hopes of a starring role.

Arthur looked at the waiters puzzled. "She wasn't expecting that she…?"

"I think you've hurt her feelings Arthur."

"But she's not a movie star, she's my assistant!"

Sophie stormed into the Crown Room and threw another script his way. It upended the tall top heavy glass, spilling the two strawberries in his lap. The 'Stuntman' balanced precariously on the edge of the table.

"Hmmm…. Is she trying to tell me something?" mused the mesmerized Arthur.

"Perhaps sir? They do replace a stunt double who is killed in the film."

"Sophie's a little inflamed, that's all" laughed Arthur.

"A woman scorned, is worse than a scorpion sting, sir."

"I suppose you're right."

"But is there anything else we can extract from the script? She has picked a lot of potential winners."

"Well if I recall sir, the film stars a charismatic director, Eli Cross played by Peter O'Toole. He helps Cameron, a fugitive on the run by hiding him in his anti-war picture. He becomes enchanted and involved with the leading lady played by Barbara Hershey. A deadly triangle develops between the three of them. Cross dares Cameron into death defying stunts which killed the previous stuntman."

"That sly Sophie!"

"But I'm the director!"

"Perhaps Miss Sophie has made other plans…"

"Other plans?"

"Why, found another director sir!"

"That's preposterous! This is my picture! My performers, my blockbuster!"

"But of course sir."

Arthur recalled the devilish Shields, the director who destroyed the others' careers only to come crawling back after blowing his attempt. He couldn't stoop that low or could he? Have her fired!"

"As you wish, sir!"

"I'll rely on my own instinct. I'll find the next Marilyn Monroe, Marlene Dietrich or Madonna if it kills me!" he fumed.

A stunning beauty dashed by, outside the doorway leading into the main chandeliered lobby; Arthur in hot pursuit.

"She's perfect!" he said disgustedly. "She fell right through my finger-tips!" He dashed to the front desk, stunned as if he'd seen a ghost.

"Excuse me, but did you see that young woman?"

"What young woman sir, we have many nervous young brides flitting about the hotel. Their last days of freedom, much like the Monarch butterfly. Until they are caught. I couldn't resist!"

"Remind me to cast you in my film."

"Why thank you sir."

"Anyway. She was about so high, didn't get a good look, but I'd recognize her if I saw her again" stammered Arthur.

"Perhaps you're feeling butterflies in the pit of your stomach before your big day?"

"What? That's preposterous!" he slobbered. "I'm not married."

"Yes, it will all be over in a few days!"

"I'm telling you I'm here on business!"

"So are the charming conniving courters, trying to add another concubine to their collection."

"Check your room records. I'm Dr Arthur. I've rented out most of this Palace."

"Oh, I'm so sorry sir."

"Let me see" as he ran his finger down the registry. He stopped at 3327 and shuddered.

"What's the matter? It's sweltering in here!"

"Nothing! Just a rumor!"

"Spit it out man!"

"In 1892 a guest, a young woman, Kate Morgan, checked into room 3312. Her estranged husband never arrived."

"How lousy, unreturned love."

"She was found dead on the beach four days later, forensics determined she had been shot."

"Tragedy."

"More than you realize, her spirit is said to roam the resort. She has been spotted on many an occasion. Quite the party or wedding crasher, yet she never utters a word. No objections."

"I tell you she was real, slightly sleazy, in a short leather mini skirt."

"That doesn't sound like our usual clientele, perhaps you are confused, mistaken her for someone else, someone you're longing for, a fiancé, a future bride?"

"That's it! I've got to lay off the spirited hot sauce for a while. It packs quite a punch."

"Might I suggest a Mocha java or rich blend of Columbian?"

"Yes, indeed, I just have to grab some fresh air. I'll take it in the 'Crown Room' thank you."

"I'll put on a fresh pot as we speak!"

Arthur loosened his tie and undid the top button from his silky sweat stained white shirt. As he stepped out admiring the sweeping view of San Diego Bay, he was mesmerized by another mirage. He rubbed his eyes in disbelief. He had had episodes of peculiar pink elephants prancing about his luxuriously landscaped property before. But a pink Cadillac? Preposterous! With giant bull horns to boot extending the entire beam of the pimp mobile. The vehicle circled the parking lot once. He couldn't believe his luck as he caught a glimpse of his elusive enchilada, in the company of such cads. Arthur felt a hint of jealousy as he raised his swordless arm, as if to challenge his foes to a fierce jousting match.

"Come back here you cowards!" you've stolen my starlet, my sweet seniorita" he yelled as he jockeyed among the stable of fine vintage vehicles and priceless collector's items parked in their personal stalls.

The plates 'Baja or Bust', the only clue, his only hope of ever encountering his buxom bodacious burrito again. The forbidden fruit, off to a foreign fiesta. The perfect picture as he framed her with both forefingers and thumbs. He was caught in a deadly dilemma. Search the streets of San Diego to find his leading lady or drop everything and follow his heart? Dash all hopes of bank rolling a block buster. He had to formulate a plan, kill two birds with one stone. How far was he willing to go in search of fame and fortune? To the ends of the earth if need be, at least to land's end. He'd raise the funds somehow he mused as he kicked a few pebbles in the parking lot. Arthur returned to the lobby.

"I saw her again."

"The ghost?"

"She's not a figment of my imagination, I swear, she's off to Mexico in a long pink Cadillac!"

The staff could not refrain from a rousing round of laughter.

"Your Columbian Coffee is waiting for you. Whenever you're ready!"

"I'm ready as I'll ever be!" said Arthur steadying the hot cup of rejuvenating java to his lips. "I'll saddle up and ride out ASAP, south of the border in search of the mother lode, the Diablo Oro. My Golden Globe goddess." The scripts were worthless without the woman.

11: Ole!

"Every country gets the circus it deserves. Spain gets bullfights. Italy gets the Catholic Church, America gets Hollywood."
- Erica Jong

Bull fighting had it's origins in Monos, in ancient Greece. The 'bull jumpers' grabbed the bull by the horns as it charged them. Many were gored. Yet there is no relation between the Spanish 'tauromachy', the killing of the sacrificial bull and the Greek event. The oldest bull ring, the El Toreo de Tijuana built entirely of wood during the prohibition era in America in the '30's was host to a semi final event. A second, the beautiful 'bullring by the sea', a post modern classic structure and second largest in Mexico was host to the other semi final event. The 'Fiestas Patronas' was performed during the annual dedica-tion to the patron saint, in this case Tijuana. The final 'big beefy burrito' is held in Mexico City later in the season.

Cali and her cool 'Columbian Cadillac Band' as she had dubbed them chose the latter ring, a taste of the new, exciting after the end of the prohibit-ion, era. They lost themselves amongst the other 21,000 blood thirsty spectators by the sea, the formidable American fenced border wall adjacent.

The first of three staged acts or Lance's Tercio was an intense observation period by the main performer, the matador He studies the bull's movements carefully to determine the direction of charge or primary horn like left or right handed-ness. The raging bull always seemed to veer to his left noted Cali.

"If he picks up on that, he can predict the bull's next move" clarified the lead singer, Jeff. "Two lancers, the picoderos on their padded steeds play with the bull. The horses, almost oblivious to the bull's tirades take the brunt of harm-less attacks. At the right moment the lancer plunged his sword into a mound of the animal's neck muscles. The first drops of blood seeped from the wound. With each strike, the animal's resistance and threatening stance was reduced.

"It's awful" It sent her to a torrid flashback of her own ominous ordeal of long ago. The fateful hook which tore through her facial muscles. How fortunate she was it had missed her carotids.

The next act entailed an exciting game of 'pin the tail on the donkey'. The three bandilleros pricked and planted two barbed sticks in the flanks of the bull. It happened fast, without much of a fight. This further weakened the neck muscles of the tiring animal. The fluttering flags were accompanied by furious erratic charges by the animal. The blood was flowing steadily from the widening gap. The crowd roared as the ensuing grand finale crept up on the unwary bull. The assistants left as the bold golden caped matador entered the bull ring. The final act, the Tercio de Muertre. The enlivened Matador stretched his cape like a taut sail and enraged the bull ever more. It passed across the matador's tracks several times ere he hoisted his muleta. He methodically maneuvered the bull to inflict the maximum thrust in the desired trajectory. Only the most skillful choreography completed the antics by piercing the animal's aorta and a clean quick death.

"Come on, Cali you love it!" coaxed her Cadillac chauffeurs. She cringed, not capable of watching the wild animal thrash around in it's death throes. He stabbed it with his steely knife but he could not kill the feisty beast. It refused to drop. As if fueled from the fiery pit itself. The barbed sticks like additional horns flailed madly. The matador's futile efforts to find the spinal chord were unnerving. The beast fought with every ounce of strength to remain standing but finally a victor emerged as the caped crusader drew his verdugo and found the mark of the beast. He spared the animal any additional pain.

"'Take a Bow' wished Cali enamored by the arduous task and tactical tenacity of the star Spanish bullfighter. The matador responded as he reeled in the roses and tossed one in her general direction, then mouthed a few flirtatious lines. She caught the red thorny twig. It pricked her finger and drew a few drops of blood.

"Say your lines but do you feel them. Do you mean what you say when no one's around?"

"A memorable video by Madonna and Emilio Munoz Non? He'll break your heart as he did Madonna. The heartbroken blonde after spending a sexually charged night with the Spanish star bullfighter, just another notorious conquest." Cali cried as a team of mules dragged the bloody loser from the forum.

"Man is the cruelest animal. At tragedies, bull-fights, and crucifixions he has so far felt best on earth. And when he invented hell for himself, it was his very heaven." (Nietsche) stated Cali.

Dr Gum seated himself in the quaint rustic old El Toreo de Tijuana along the Agua Caliente, the oldest road and most strategic point in the tourist trap. Dr Arthur had followed the trail of the pink panther as it parked but was impeded by all the people parading through the streets during the 'Fiesta Patronas'. He chose the older building as well. The peculiar chapel aside the old wooden structure startled him. Certainly not the traditional chapel he'd hope to marry his future wife in. The culture shock continued as he met a matador kneeled in a moment of silence inside.

"Que pasa?" humored Arthur as he kneeled next to the bull fighter.

"Please, I must pay my respects, my prayer, perhaps my last rights" he said ominously. Arthur said his hail mary's and prayed he'd find his feisty female lead for his film."

"Why is someone sick or going to die? Aren't you supposed to be happy? You're the brave matador, the bull should be in here on all fours, and that's no bull!"

The matador cracked a faint smile.

"I always get butterflies in the pit of my stomach before a mano-a-mano."

"Man no…?"

"A head to head battle between two cunning bull fighters. There's much more at stake than meets the eye. Certainly the animal will die but my honor will be bruised, tarnished, even torn apart if I lose to an amateur matador."

"You're taking this much too seriously" slurred Arthur. "I'll buy you a marguerita at the festival this evening. Wash away your worries and enjoy the mariachi bands. And other international talent."

"Si senor, wash away my sorrows, an 'anointing of the sick' so to speak!"

"Si, now stick it to them sport!" said Arthur equally thirsty for the alluring alcoholic beverages as the bull's blood. Perhaps he'd find his feisty female star in the local cantina tonight? Dr Arthur and Dr Gum and were seated on opposite ends of the spectrum in the stylish Spanish bull ring. The two matadors took a deep bow for the boisterous spectators. The elder experienced matador kept his hat on during his pasaille or parade. The younger rookie removed his hat out of respect. They were each to tackle three bulls, in this afternoon matinee. The Pride of Mexico, Pedro Gonzalez and the Tijuana Tiger, Garcia Sanchez. Arthur recognized the 2nd man in this dynamic duel. He wondered if his prayers would be answered as his own? The bullfighter who has the extraordinary ability to do with the bull what creates the intensest emotion from the spectators will depend upon the animal to charge." (Ernest Hemingway, Death in the Afternoon, 1932)

"Bullfighting, a whole lotta bull but even bigger balls exhibited by the bull fighters" nudged Dr Gum to his neighborly nachos munching Mexicans. The fan belched and cracked a toothless grin as he gulped down his Corona cooler. The two fighters fought valiantly through the first two rounds or acts. A surprise sneak attack by the steaming mad bull caught Garcia off guard. The horn hooked him under the rib cage and gored his lung. He collapsed gasping for breath. The spectators rose to their feet screaming. Unable to get up, the beast charged and stomped on the helpless hurting bull fighter. The bull continued to crush the cranium concealed under the bloody black beaten hat. A local Spanish doctor rushed into the ring as the padded horseback riders routed the raging bull into an enclosure. There was nothing he could do to revive him. His lifeless body was dragged to the edge of his stage, leaving a dusty rut down the middle of the ring. The surprise performance his last.

"My God" muttered Arthur. He needed a stiff tequila to kill the painful images perfusing his mind. "Did you see that?" he asked the amused enchiladas next to him.

"He had it coming to him gringo" having fooled around with everyone of them, the determined Don Juan had met his match.

"Good riddence" shouted the scorned senoritas.

"Excuse me" said Arthur as he escaped the cheering crowd, as remorseful as the Romans in their coliseum he figured. He'd have to watch his step in this town he fretted. Perhaps making a movie here was not such a brilliant idea?

"What am I doing here anyway?" His woes ended as he stepped to the perimeter of the ring. In the distance, a pink pimple stuck out like a sore thumb. It kicked up a cloud of debris as it rolled down a dusty side road toward a tiny cantina, 'The Thirsty Iguana'. He made his way back to his Mercedes 450 SL. It had acquired a few extra racing stripes sitting for the three acts. A few wires dangled under the dash where his Blaupunkt stereo once hung. Fortunately they did not fire up his beautiful fire engine red beast.

"No point in putting up the bonnet" said Arthur. He turned the key hesitantly, hunching his head. Luckily it started without an accompanying explosion, a constant threat from the drug cartels. I've been watching too many murder mysteries mused Arthur shaking his head. He laughed out loud still in shock as he coasted to the cantina. He wiped the perspiration from his brow and breathed a sigh of relief as he swung the saloon doors. A shapely Spanish waitress approached him in the darkened dance hall.

"Tequila?"

"Terrific. That's music to my ears

"The band doesn't start 'til 9 PM"

"That's one sarcastic seniorita" he stated. She led him through the maze of Mexican lounge lizards then seated him at a table for two near the stage.

"Gracios."

"Si senor." Arthur was temporarily relieved, removed from the rat race. He'd escaped his ever present entourage. Never a prisoner of his own device but the vengeful vultures persistently preyed on his pesos. He noticed a somber majestically attired fellow at the next table.

"Excuse me, but aren't you Pedro? Pedro Gonzalez?"

"Si."

"I'm sorry for your loss, I mean your amigo. I'm Arthur."

The waitress hovered close to the stage in anticipation of the new band from Hollywood.

"Tequila Stuntman" suggested Pedro. The woman complied and brought a bottle of 'gold' a few slices of lemon and a shaker of salt.

"Uno duo tres" the two men in a fierce duel snorted a pile of salt from the back of their hands slammed the glass down their gullets, then squirted the lemon juice in each other's eyes. A few shots and they were in tears, sobbing like babies.

"He was my amigo since I was old enough to whack my piñata. All the other assistants, I do not care for. They are simply there to await the spoils, carve up the beast. Garcia had guts, he had to bring down the animal almost single handedly every time!"

"It's a crying shame" slurred Arthur as he slammed the empty tequila bottle on the rickety table. "My staff would probably stab me in the back given the first opportunity. We're all just prisoners here of our own device."

"No."

"Si" The waitress quickly snatched the bottle before he'd shatter it into a million pieces.

"Permit me, a Slammer Royale, a bottle of your best! pronto!"

"Si!" said the woman excitedly.

"I know the Slammer, but the Royale is rare around here!"

"Relax, Pedro, tonight we celebrate, to commemorate friendship, and future fortunes to be made!" The waitress promptly placed a bottle of Dom Perignon and another Tequila Gold in the center of the round wooden table. The other patrons wondered who this wealthy wayfarer was as he pried the cork from the Dom. It popped and sailed through the air and bounced off the snare drum. Arthur concocted an equal part tequila and Champagne leaving about a fifth empty for the fizz. He slammed it on the table then downed it rapidly. The contents exploded in his mouth then swallowed the sweet drink. The champagne rapidly raced through his systemic circulation.

"Any plans Pedro? Do you want to be in pictures?"

"You mean the movies?"

"No, I mean Corona pitchers." Pedro burst into tears of laughter and nearly pissed himself.

"Of course I mean films, the big screen. There's so few of us chivalrous conquistadors left, you know!"

"Si! Senor you've got that right."

"I'm shooting a film, "Some Like it Hot! or something like that."

"You've come to the right place. It's almost 100 degrees around here every day in the summers."

"Ha, ha, ha, " roared Arthur oblivious to all others around him.

"Hey buddy, the bands about to begin, can you keep it down?"

Cali walked onto the stage accompanied by her cool stray cats, They were introduced individually as 'Cali and the Cadillac Crooners' each in a pseudo blues brother's attire with the dark framed sunglasses and hats. They began their set with 'Wastin' away again in Margueritaville'; it was when the line ‘some people say that there’s a woman to blame’ But I know it’s no-body’s fault, (Hell it could be my fault) (It’s my own damn fault)’ that Arthur recognized his saucy seniorita from San Diego! He was so shocked he dropped his shooter glass and interrupted their song.

“You’re my shining star!” he slurred, interrupting her lines.

“If you don’t knock it off buddy you’ll be seeing stars and stripes” recognizing his California accent

“How about a song for my pal Pedro, over here?” he pleaded. The irritated muscle bound patron approached Arthur. Something stirred deep inside Cali

“It’s OK, I know just the tune.”

“Sure?”

“I’m sure.”

“One more wise crack out of you…”

Cali boldly began ‘Last night I dreamt of San Pedro….’ The band quickly caught on. She finished a few bars ‘Tropical the island breeze all of nature wild and free that’s where I long to be…and when the samba played…..
your Spanish lullaby.” She brought the house

down. She was an instant smash with the sloshed patrons and staff.

"Bravo, bravo" applauded Arthur before he fell flat on his face at Cali's feet. He hit his chin nearly knocking out an entire row of teeth. The jealous jock belted him with a hook and broke his nose and glass, then grabbed Arthur and flung him across the stage. He pierced the skin of the conga drum. His arm was wedged with his face unable to free himself as the band scattered. The audience was in tears at the antics of this ridiculous amusing amigo as he stood up. He bounced into the other instruments upsetting the entire ensemble. The bouncer grabbed him by his congas and tossed him out the back door. He rolled down the alley alerting a few passers by. Dr Gum amongst them rushed to his aid and pried the drum from his head.

"Dr Arthur…. Sperry?"

"Dr Gum? What a pleasant surprise."

"I always knew you danced to the tune of a different drum, but…"

"It's a long story, ouch, I think it's broken" he mumbled.

"I've got to get you to a hospital ASAP." He

examined his teeth. You might need some reconstructive work."

"What an introduction!"

"Just who were you trying to impress this time?"

"Marilyn, my movie star…"

"Monroe?….I think you've had one too many margueritas…."

"Thanks Arthur, Adios" said his dream girl as she strode off in Pedro's arms" as he passed out.

12: Body Shots

"Beauty is in the eye of the beholder. "
- Margaret Hungerford

"Where's my Marilyn? I demand to know!" bellowed the obnoxious boozer. Arthur awoke somewhere in Mexico in a hospital."

"You are lucky your friend bailed you out, or you'd have spent the night in the TJ slammer!" said the ER surgeon.

"What happened?" he asked incoherently, having difficulty with his speech. His arm was in a cast and sling.

"How are you feeling?" asked Dr Gum as he leaned over his colleague.

"Like a stuffed tequila at thanksgiving, or is that

turkey?"

"I think he's fine. Thanks Dr Sanchez."

"I'll give you three choices."

"Oh I like games" said Arthur able to form a few consonants.

"You can see Dr Topete in Guada-lajara, Dr Flores in Lima. They both have a prominent patient base. You might even find a female lead for your movie? I've let them know you'll stop by. They can help you put your teeth back in time."

"In time for what?"

"For the Bisbee's tournament. I see you've lost your phenomenal memory. You know, lands' end!"

'This is the end, my friend' kept ringing through Arthur's mind, the eerie Jim Morrison melody.

"I must be off! Mosey on, slowly make my way down Baja to Cabos."

"Don't close the door! That's only two. Who's on third?"

"Dr Pitanquay in Brazil. If you can't find what you're looking for. Adios."

"Adios" Baja? He kept repeating the two syllables. Suddenly it came back to him. "or bust!" he blurted out.

Arthur decided on the short jaunt to Guadalajara across the Gulf Of California. A hop skip and a jump from Cabos to compete in the challenge. The word was mum about his misfortunes, to any prying staff eyes and ears, including Sophie. He was here simply to relax and regain his composure as far as they were concerned, a covert operation incognito. He'd only divulge his true intentions to Cali, that is if he'd ever find her again. Arthur checked into the posh post modern Guadalajara clinic of Dr Topete; a colleague of Dr Gum's.

"Ah, my amigo, buenas dias! You are my prized patient." His warmth and charm extended to everyone, always referred to as 'my patient'.

"Buenos Nachos" mumbled Arthur. The liquid lunch, a number of small bottles onboard Aero Mexico, had anaesthetized him adequately. He did not need any local other than a shot of nitrous.

"I'm going to place a few implantsand place an entire arch of beautiful porcelain sculpted teeth over them, si?"

"See, I can barely speak or move!"

"Just sign here."

Arthur fumbled with the pen in his left, his other writing arm comfortably cushioned in the massive cast.

"You know, the earliest teeth were simply sea shells sculpted by the talented Mayan artisan, set in the empty bony sockets. We are proud of our ancestors accomplishments Arthur."

"Ahhh" nodded Arthur in agreement non coherently floating from the inhalant, nitrous oxide. Arthur's gums were pierced, the implants were placed precisely into his upper tooth socket voids. A set of choppers, individually sculpted from pearly white porcelain were mounted atop. Arthur came around after about an hour.

"See!" The Top Doc offered Arthur a hand held mirror.

"Mirror, mirror on the wall ..." laughed Arthur sorely. "Si!" he accepted his new appearance appreciatively.

"You'll have to be careful, No steaks for a few weeks while the implants heal. Gradually you'll learn to grind, grit your teeth, and learn to speak again. I suggest soft burritos and milkshakes for a while." Arthur set the mirror down and studied the fair maidens on the wall.

"Many of my famous patients" stated the implantologist proudly.

Arthur was in awe by a blond bombshell and approached a few of her photos.

"Ah, a stunning beauty, Dolores Del Rio. Ushered in during our 'Golden Age of Cinema in Mexico in the 1940's. Unfortunately Hollywood films did not fan out south of the border. The numerous Spanish dialects were difficult to translate and comprehend by the Mexicans."

"Ah, gooo, gah …."

She had the opportunity to star amongst many of the greatest. The Charlie Chaplin of Mexico", Mario Moreno so dubbed by your own legend Charlie Chaplin, who considered him the greatest comedian in the world. The impoverished comedian rose from the streets in the slums to become the symbol of the people, the Underdog, a verbal innovator with universal appeal."

"Iquita gree."

"Some felt he was nothing more than a bourgeois puppet"

Arthur reflected on his own position in life,

floundering around lately.

"Del Rio married MGM's Cedric Gibbons in 1930, a magnificent art director and producer. In 1941, Orson Welles fell madly in love with her, tearing her away from Gibbons in divorce.

"I can hee hy."

"So can I" stated Dr Topete confused. "They collaborated on a film together 'Journey Into Fear' in 1942, which later influenced a Bond film 'From Russia with Love' The protagonist, not a profess-ional spy, was underestimated It featured satanic Nazi operatives, Bulgarian assassins, A Spanish courtier and pimp and a French couple."

"Now you're awking."

"Ah yes, here in 'Flying down to Rio" in 1933" Dr Topete pointed to a pair of dancers.

"Hed Ast air and Injur Ogurs."

"Yes, it was Fred Astaire and Ginger Roger's first dance together on film. To the 'Carioca, which won Best Song at the Academy Awards. Astaire plays an accordion player in an orchestra led by a successful script writer Roger Bond (Gene Raymond). Bond falls for a Brazillian bombshell (Del Rio) and is therefore fired. He gets a gig in Brazil nevertheless, where a few shady businessmen are blocking the opening of a new hotel. Bond marries the Brazilian, the hotel opens."

Tears welled up in Arthur's eyes.

"There, there Arthur" consoled the clinician. "He knew what he wanted and went for it."

"Egg zack lee."

"In 1960, she was in 'Flaming Star' with this gaucho." Dr T. pointed to the personality on horseback in the vast spread.

"That El iss."

"Yes Elvis, in one of his best performances as 'Pacer Burton' a half-breed born to a Texas cattle rancher and Kiowa woman. The neighboring tribe is attacking the homesteads. He is torn between two worlds, belonging to neither." Arthur assumed he might succumb to a similar fate. Forfeiting his fortunes if he pursued his elusive en-chanting enchilada. But love is blind!

"The Kiowa allied with the Cheyenne and Apaches and fought eastern tribes. In the 'Treaty of Medicine Lodge' of 1867, the Kiowa were forced to settle on a reserve by the US military. Chief Santana, 'White bear' was taken captive but jumped to his death from a 2nd story window in the prison."

"O I God!" gasped Arthur.

"Are you all right Arthur?"

"Fine."

Dr Topete and his alluring assistant escorted Arthur and his free arm to the last set of frames.

"Sara Garcia, a legend of more than 140 movies mostly known for her' granny' roles. At 22 she appeared in her first film when Azteca Films was shooting in Mexico City. Her screening led to several cinema productions and an act in a theater company 'Compana de Comedia Selecta'. Later she starred with legend remember Mario Moreno?"

"Si!" Arthur nodded his head.

"The longest running telenovela in Latin America, 'Munde de Juguete' stars Garcia as Christina, Mariano's daughter, a widower. She drifts off into a world of her own (munde de juguete) yet manages to find a wife for her father who remarries."

Arthur nearly stumbled over a leather sofa in the consult area as he saw the next nearly naked nacho.

"In the 1980's the 'Sexicomedias' starred

Sasha Montenegro , the queen of these B comedies, one of the sexiest of all time with her role in the telenovela 'un mujer murcado'. (A Tainted Woman).

Though thoroughly amused, these actresses, although equally talented and alluring, were all dead. Arthur knew he had found a gold mine, with his Golden Globe goddess.

"She's all mine!" stated Arthur slipped off into a fantasy film world.

The assistant gently placed Arthur in the sumptuous leather cushions. He sank into a short soothing sleep instantly. His thoughts drifted to the decadent beaches of Rio de Janeiro, The scantily clad fashion models, the movie stars, the hookers, the prostitutes, all the women who relied on their good looks to make a prosperous living. They could all afford the complete costly makeovers. In the hands of the gifted surgeon, Ivo Pitanguy, they became his canvas as he carefully applied his artistic abilities. The world renown plastic surgeon sculpted their sagging saddle bags, remolded their aging arches, restored their shapely figures to propel them into prosperous careers as future film stars, high priced models with their hourglass figures and high cheek bones. Even the prostitutes and hookers received a boost to their bawdy life styles in the brothels and sex starved streets.

Arthur imagined himself amongst his hot harem on a steamy beach. Their bronzed bodies, dripping with the aromatic oils which he delicately massaged into their toned tanned torsos. He straddled each enticing enchilada in turn, easing their tension. After all his tropic tan sports illustrated illusions had rolled over they asked Arthur to take your best shot. No cameras were present. Each woman had a slice of lemon waiting between her luscious red lips. Their heads were turned. A shooter glass balanced between their bikini bound breasts. Arthur knew what to do grabbing a handful of grains from a sugary mountain next to him on the beach. He licked each of their necks in turn, then sprinkled the sugar onto their moistened necks. He grabbed the tequila shooter glass from their sternum and greedily gulped the contents. He hurriedly placed a piece of lemon between each pair of luscious red lips then sucked the juice from their mouths. Arthur came to the last woman.

It was the intoxicating image of Cali, her soft smooth complexion and enticing eyes melted any memory of the succulent sweet dishes decked out on the deserted beach.

"Why Caligula? Why am I always the last? Can you not assuage your amorous antics?" How could she equate him to the monster? Albeit Arthur's extravagance eccentricity, and desperate depravity at times attained a Caligula-like lecherousness. He was certainly no monster! Perhaps it was a warning, a premonition? After all, the demented emperor had met his death at the hands of his own men. At least 30 fatal stab wounds in the back and groin. The haunting image of Cali shocked him, sending him instantly into the realm of consciousness. He leaned up and fell back off the leather couch, and tumbled onto the terra cotta tiled floor.

"Arthur, Arthur, are you alright?" as his assistant doused him with her Perrier water bottle.

"You must have had quite a bad dream. There, there poor baby" said the astute Latin American attendant comforted Arthur and placed his head between her ample artificial breasts. He regained his composure, somewhat woozy. Clutching a marvelous juicy melon, about to take a bite from the forbidden fruit.

"Whoa, those cost me a pretty penny" said Stacy. Dr Pitanguy always warned me to watch out for sharp objects, he didn't mention teeth."

"So sorry, Stacy" excused Arthur, I don't want you to spring a leak! I was in the middle of a wild dream with beautiful bikini clad calendar girls all around. I caressed each one of them then consumed the contents of shooter glasses balancing on their …."

"I get the picture. Perhaps I should be more careful? Have them replaced with the newer silicone? What do you think?"

"You look fine!"

"Si" said Dr Topete, more concern-ed with Arthur's adverse reaction to the nitrous oxide. Or simply the shock and trauma from the incident, either way he had to remain under close observation for the time being.

"I don't think I'll fly to Rio, but if my future wife ever asks about a little enhancement, I'll be sure to send her south for the winner. The plastic surgeon's hands have created a truly beautiful creature. You're spectacular Stacy" said Arthur as if presenting an award for best special effects in cinematography and motion pictures. Even his speech seemed more articulate.

"Why thank you, but I want to play it safe on the playa."

"No piercings, particularly the nipple!" pleaded Arthur facetiously.

"Ha, ha, ha" the three amigos attained a concerted comical hearty roar of laughter.

"You sure, there isn't a nitrous leak in here somewhere, I feel wired!" wondered Arthur.

"I don't think so Arthur, it's your contagious comical style. You really ought to be in pictures"

"Perhaps Stacy can play a saucy spicy assistant in another sexicomedia, a satirical look at double entendres and insinuendos?"

"Would you care to invest a few pesos in the picture?"

"Perhaps!"

"We haven't had that spirit here since 1969!" said Stacy. Arthur's mind was reeling. The last thing Arthur remembered was walking to the door, he had to find the passage back to the place he was before! Take a Tijuana taxi if he had to, scour all the sordid haunts to find his true starlet.

13: La Paz

"Human beings, indeed all sentient beings, have the right to pursue happiness and live in peace and freedom."
- XIVth Dalai Lama

Dr Gum felt relieved to get out of the smoke infested hacienda inhabited by the irritable lounge lizards. He strolled along the tranquil seaside resort in La Paz, Spanish for peace. He'd soon put the large modern 'Dove of Peace Monument' sculpture at the gateway to the city to the test. It's translated inscription reads 'And if you want peace, I offer it to you in the sunny peace of my bay.' The only war Dr Gum planned to wage, if necessary in the shallow waters, was a mano-a-mano with the temperamental high strung snappers. They usually proved to be the victors in the violent struggles, dubbed the 'hope-less snapper'. Even the most experienced seasoned angler with his assortment of live sardines, or flat iron herring as bait, with up to 200 lb test line proves futile in the fight. Most days are spent simply dropping a line, then soaking up the rays until a rapid reply awakens the wary fisherman. It can be 'heaven or hell' anticipating, waiting for the first tug of a lively red snapper, mullet snapper, a big cabrillo or leopard grouper or an even bigger dog snapper. The lush green plankton carpet lining the nutrient rich reclusive region created a formidable collection from the smallest ornamental species up to the mammoth 1000 pound marlin. With everything conceivable in between, Dorado- mahi-mahi, Yellow fin Tuna, and Sailfish. The perfect preamble to the 'Big Event' in Cabos only a couple of days away. The most difficult choice in the challenge, or 'duel' was a choice of venue. To the north of the city, fishing focused around the Isla Espiritu Santo and a nearby neighbor Isla Partido. To the south, about an hour away was the Punta Arena de la Ventana, an idyllic 'Bay of Dreams' (Bahia de Suenos). The bay conceals a deadly secret, it's former ominous name, the 'Ensenada de los Muertos'. Dr Gum and his limited Spanish did not want to venture anywhere near the 'Bay of the Dead'. He'd thought it best to let it rest in peace as he motioned his panga guide to prepare to cast off. The mid size cruiser set out for a cluster of small rocky projections off shore. An ideal locale for lazing away the afternoon loung -ing around on the deck. Kick back a few Coronas and cast your cares away. The endless hours of boredom marked by seconds of sheer terror. Much like the life of an anaesthe-tist, as they waited the first signs of eagerly awaited marine life.

"Where are they hiding?" asked Dr Gum. "Perhaps that is what they meant by 'Bay of the Dead'? Not a peep from the sly snappers. In the spring these waters are teeming with life as the snappers toss and turn spawning on the rocks in only 10 feet of water. The panga guide heaved some anchor chain into the water as we found another prime spot, followed by 200 lb. test line to avoid sheering the line on the sharp rocks. The waiting game initially taxed my patience, then turned into an extremely relaxing afternoon if I don't say so myself. My thoughts drifted to poor Dr Arthur. He'd likely miss all the action in his rigid confining plaster cast. Yet he was a prisoner of his own device, the drinking binges were lasting longer, he was slowly losing the battle. In fact, he was totally out of control. Everything in moderation and temperance thought Dr Gum as he tossed back another Budweiser. It was his choice, but he hated to see a colleague self destruct.

"I have to do something" snapped Dr Gum out loud.

"Relax doc" there's nothing you can do now but wait."

"Oh, I was just lost in thought."

"Don't worry, be happy! We've got all the time in the world." Dr Gum felt time was slowly running out for his alcoholic alumnus, yet Dr Arthur wasn't dead yet!

"Doc, STAT!" snapped the pango guide. Dr Gum eagerly awaited the yank on his rod. He relished the challenge, methodically mastering the motion with each additional outing, gaining valuable intuition. The type of fish, their characteristic tactic, the type of tackle. It was all falling into place, his persistence was beginning to pay off. Soon he'd see the whites of their eyes. Just one more yank! He felt victory slip through his fingertips as the tension in his rod and reel suddenly ceased. A few flowery Spanish expletive deletives emanated from his experienced entourage. No matter, there were plenty more fish where that came from.

"We'll see who has the last laugh, si senor?"

"Si, Rodriguez." No sooner had he said, it that he snagged another feisty foe. The scaly snapper fought like a dog, but in the end, expired. Dr Gum had out wrangled the ornery denison of the deep. He heaved the huge dog snapper onto the deck amongst the other out muscled prisoners. A few more rounds, and the casualty count mounted. A mountain of snappers fit for suateing were stacking up in the stern of the boat. The odds were certainly in their favor, nearly playing with a full deck as the day drew to a close.

"A full house. I have to thank my crew. I

couldn't have done it without you" congratulated the aching gringo. Dr. Gum gripped each of their hands, offering a firm handshake.

"Gracios, captain Gum."

"If this is any indication of what's in store, or prelude to the fiesta resistance, I'll be mighty pleased" he said proud of his Mexican marauders.

"Si, si, gracios!" They admired their amigo, potentially the new admiral on the block.

"To top off such a splendid day" as he eyed the collection of cabrillo, mullet and snapper "calls for a celebration, a corona for one and all" as he offered each a bottle of the best. The chunks had melted as he reached into the ice cold water; as did any doubts about his angling ability.

"Wait!" said Rodriguez as he raised his hand. He fished around in the icy cooler and found a plump round lemon. In one swift motion he sliced several strips with the stiletto he found in his fishing vest.

"Squeeze!" He urged his com-padres. The chilled contents went down real smooth. Good to the last drop. They each downed two coronas, then attempted to haul in the heavy anchor.

"Here, let me help you Pedro, you're obviously

already drunk!"

His partner pulled the particularly peculiar poundage onto the bow.

"I'm getting too old for this!" he insisted.

"Nah, you've been out on the water all day. You just need a plate of nutritious nachos and a nubile nymph to energize you."

"I'll drive" insisted Dr Gum as he took the helm, then fixated on the distant harbor lights.

"Are you sure you can drive this tugboat? You've had two coronas. It's not good to drink and drive" he laughed boisterously.

"Are you kidding? They don't call me Captain La Paz for nothing" he said presumptuously. He felt he could catch any flounderer now. "Let's see what she's got."

"Si, senor you're the boss."

Dr Gum gunned the throttle and kicked up quite a wake roaring across the bay.

"Hey amigo, all's well that ends well." Dr Gum grabbed one end of the heavy cooler, crammed with all kinds of scaly specimens. A cargo worth it's weight in gold figured Dr Gum

"We'll filet them and file them into the freezer

later. For the time being we'll spend our fortune. He tossed them each several large bills and a couple of pesos, all the spare change he had.

"Now where's the best cantina in town? You've earned it" he rejoiced enthusiastically.

"Gracious Dr Gum"

"Well let's see" Sanchez scratched his head as he started the ignition to his top down jeep. Most of the night life lay along the malecon at the water's edge. But he'd give Dr Gum a little extra side tour, fewer choices than Cabos, but he'd let the captain call the shots. The others placed their collection into their hats and wore them proudly on their heads. He circled around town a few times, passing the Hotel Palmira and Gran Baja, two discoteques with live music and dancing.

"Mucho musicanto!" remarked Ricardo squashed like a sardine in the middle of the back seat. Sanchez taxied in a wider perimeter passing a few local artisans shops, Artesania Cuauhtemoc, 'The Weaver' of fine hand woven woolen goods. His circumference closed as he swooped in on the central downtown district. La Perla de La Paz, a pricey upper end establishment of enticing fine merchandise appeared.

"Let's go to the 'Grill'" suggested Garcia.

"You're always eating!" exclaimed Pedro.

"Keep an eye on the lid or he'll help himself to some sushi" ribbed Sanchez.

"No, I meant the Grill Xtasis and Video bar."

"Si, a spectacular laser light show. You like senor?"

"Si. Let's see what the excitement is all about!" as they pulled up to the loud locale, laser lights bouncing and rebounding everywhere as they entered.

"Wow!" The captain caught a glimpse of the gyrating girls as they shook their booty in time to the bright beams and the booming bass beat.

"This dazzling display albeit illuminating is giving me a headache."

"Si, we need something slightly slower pace" suggested Rodriguez.

"Silencio" shouted Sanchez, getting tired of playing chauffeur. He was paid to fish. But he knew where to find...."Follow me!" he said as he stormed out of the light show. The women's eyes wander-ed off stage inspecting the slippery seamen that got away. The jeep circled back to the calming breakers crashing onto the seashore.

"We'll walk" he said softly listening to the sounds of silence. The consortium strolled down the beach boulevard. A Spanish guitar began to strum ever so softly in the distance. It's soothing lullaby nearly put the sailors to sleep. Suddenly the brass section started, two trumpets formed a faster frenzy of blasts. Two violins filled the void, while a guilleron, a small side bass kept the steady beat alive. To round out the rising crescendo of the consuming mariachi melody a vibrillon and high pitched stringed guitar. The music mesmerized the quintet, reeling them in. A serenade of happy Spanish tunes enticed the pairs of lovebirds seated around the perimeter of the open air terrace. 'Dulces Suenos' (Sweet Dreams in spanish) a picturesque seaside restaurant and nightclub, normally noted for it's romantic interludes. Much like the Plaza de los Mariachi's a Guadalajara, where the mariachi bands began. Whether to serenade a seniorita, trying to win her heart, or woo a 'mother or inlaw on mother's day; the enchanting tunes usually took their toll.

Touching memories, even tears of joy as the jubilant bandoleros broke the resistance of any apprehensive admirer. The 'buskers' (Spanish- to seek) or street performers accomplished their purpose, as they sought to bring loved ones together. The enchanting bars echoed off into the distance, lost in the breakers as they pounded onto the shore.

"It's perfect!" said Dr Gum. He preferred a table for two, in this idyllic setting for a romantic tryst. The seniorita's sensual perfumes blended with a soothing sea breeze. The fishermen did not need to lure their affection, after all their lurid wives waited patiently for them to bring home the 'big fish'. He was always the odd man out, the single spoke, the fifth wheel about to wander off the main road. In stead he was burdened by his crusty crew in tow, their salty sweat drenched tee shirts stunk. The entire lot of them best left to linger sorting fish bait or skinning the slippery scaly specimens in a sea side shack. But he had promised to share a piece of the prosperity with them. A few pesos to soothe their parched thirsty throats. The waiter seated them off in the corner of the courtyard, down wind.

"Corona?" questioned the cocky waiter.

"Tequila!" retorted Rodriguez. "A bottle of the best. Doc's orders." The waiter brought the house brand, Tequila Gold and five shooter glasses. The bait, the worm, was bobbing and wobbling in the bottle.

"To the king's crew" toasted Dr Gum. "May the joy juice in your gizzard keep you warm in a blizzard and may the vultures and the buzzards never gitcha'"

"The startled Spaniards looked at each other, they did not understand.

"What is blizzard?"

"A snowstorm!"

"Snow?"

"White powder?….to ski on."

They wiped their brows, worrying at the mere mention of the word.

"Why so sad?"

"We want no part of the war, between rival drug lords and cartels."

"Rumor has it, their tentacles have reached as far north as La Paz."

“We have seen strange things.”

“Strange things? you sure it isn’t the tequila talking?” asked Dr Gum

“No senor Gum, it is the midnight mariners…”

“Si, they must be mad! dumping their gutted bait into the Gulf of California and even in the bay. They never hang around to reap the rewards.”

”You sure you’re not imagining all this?” humored Dr Gum.“ Your ghost story sounds like a lot of guac (amoli) to me.”

“We’ve never actually found any traces…”

“Well you’ve seen how feisty the snappers are around here, they work up quite an appetite tang-ling with the likes of you gringos, fish have to eat too. Don’t you think they’d rather eat than be eaten?”

“Si, senor, you’re one humorous amigo.”

“But one day we’ll get to the bottom of this, right gringos?”

“Si Sanchez.”

“You see, we’ve been fishing off these shores for centuries just like our forefathers did. We have adopted many proven methods.”

“I’ll drink to that, to the tequila tacklers” he toasted as the mariachis made their rounds to their table.

“Tonight you drown your troubles in tequila and dream of tomorrow” insisted the members of the mariachi band. Their haunting melodies lingered in the lonely streets of La Paz.

14: A Hook?

"I may be a living legend but that sure don't help when I have to change a flat tire."

- Roy Orbison

Dr Topete assessed Dr Arthur's lack of concentration, it had him very concerned. He was certainly in no condition to drive.

"Tell you what" suggested Eduardo. "Stacy, you have about two weeks off coming up, don't you?"

"Yes, but…"

"No buts. I'd like you to accompany Arthur to

Cabos as his private nurse, all expenses paid."

"That sounds like a great idea. Thanks." She wrapped her arms around her boss and gave him a big bear hug.

"Don't thank me, thank Arthur, after all if Dr Gum hadn't referred him to us…" Stacy reached around to embrace Arthur but found it futile, his big cast always got in the way.

"We're off to the races!" humored Arthur appreciative of the personalized attentive care.

**

Stacy at the helm, the cherry red Mercedes Benz headed south on Mexico #1 D. About 29 km south of Tijuana, the small town of Rosarito, flourished, estab-lished in 1927, The Rosarito Beach Hotel a favorite secluded fly-in spot for an ass-ortment of Hollywood legends. Stacy dreamed of leaving her employer Eduardo, even if it had taken her twenty years to earn her prominent post. It was time for a cool change. A golden opportunity seemed to have dropped into her lap. "I can't blow this!" she mused, as David Lee Roth rambled on about how he wished 'they all could be California Girls'. Arthur intent on procuring a blockbuster, whatever the cost, began to craft a role for his escort. They arrived in Ensenada, during the prohibition in the 1920's, it became the frequented gambling and drinking destination for prominent show people.

"No time to linger" stated Stacy eyeing the one armed lounge lizard fumbling with a few maps with his free hand. The astute assistant did not want to gamble on their lengthy road trip on the #1 south so she pulled into a petrol station. She grabbed a squeegee and soaked herself removing the grit and dust that had accumulated on the short trip so far. Arthur simply sat back and soaked in the scenery. The soapy water bottle spray awoke him from his delicious desert dream.

"Time to motor, man!" she said intent on getting on the road again. Unfortunately her timing was a little off. The mid day traffic was irritating as they converged on the Plaza Civica. The three large busts, about 12 feet high, in 'Three Heads Park' startled her. The freedom fighters of Mexico, Father Miguel Hidalgo, and former Presidents Benito Juarez and Venustiano Carranza gave her the creeps. She felt they were ogling her as the traffic came to a snail's crawl pace.

A band from the neighboring base preparing for a performance thoroughly confused her bearings as she headed south east.

"At last, hasta la vista" she waved weaving out of the waning traffic as she left the outskirts of town. The intense desert sun beat down upon the solitary travelers relentlessly as they sailed along the extremely arid desert environment. Her soaked casual white uniform gave her little comfort. Stacy's zipper continued to inch earthward. Her cleavage clearly in view as Arthur pointed to the mountain peaks.

"Pick achoo …del Diablo" he said pointing to his left above her shoulder.

"Gesundheit" acknowledged Stacy.

"What?"

"I hope you don't catch cold you poor thing" She noticed the perspiration dripping from the end of his bulky cast.

"Del Diablo, the devil's peak, the tallest mound in Baja!"

"Oh, I ….."

"Thanks, it's the thought that counts" cheering her up. They pulled over high atop a hill next to a shrine providing a panoramic picturesque view of the town of San Felipe and the yellow sandy beaches below from the 940 foot promontory.

"How romantic, Muldoon's point" said Stacy as she stretched her aching limbs, limbering.

"Virgin...

"Arthur? Aren't you being a little naughty!"

"Of Guadeloupe, the shrine" he said fumbling with the map, then dropped it to the floor.

He reached down to retrieve it as Stacy leaned over revealing some spectacular scenery of her own. Their heads smacked together, both seeing stars.

"Holy guacamole" said Arthur holding his aching head.

"How clumsy of me!" she said "let me kiss it better!" fearing she'd blown her audition.

"That's quite alright, Stacy, you drive me crazy, but you'll kill me before I'll ever get this picture completed."

"I was just trying to help!"

"It is the perfect spot for a picture."

"Why don't you take a few photos of me?" she

pleaded as she peeled off her white wrapping. Her alluring multicolored tropical floral tonga had Arthur flustered as he fumble with the fish lens viewfinder. Stacy's ample features filled the entire frame. Miraculously he clicked a shot.

"We need a tripod" she snapped.

"There'll be plenty more photo ops" said Arthur, whose temperature was rising. He began to reel staggering around about to tumble off the hilltop. Stacy caught him and reeled him into her arms. His private nurse eased him into the passenger seat and strapped him in. Arthur drifted off into a tempting tropical daydream, with his budding bodacious beach beauty. She was wining him over, in his albeit unique talent search. Stacy boldly went where most women had not gone before as they entered the "Valley of the Giants' an intriguing sight. A cluster of huge cardon cacti rose from the roughening roadside. She pulled over as Arthur awoke. He was momentarily startled then realized their big mistake.

"We're going the wrong way!"

"What?"

"We're on the #3, we must've taken a wrong turn

in Ensenada. We can't go on. We have to go back." he said disgustedly. "Women drivers!" he fumed

"I'm such a clumsy fool!"

"It's not your fault, I'm the navigator" he laughed.

"I was leading you on to God know's where…"

"We'll simply back track and start anew. Agreed?"

"Agreed." She shook his free hand jiggling her amazing artificial mounds of jello.

"Take two!" joked Arthur "scene two, let's take it from the top!""

They circled back, the treacherous torture test was taking it's toll on the Mercedes convertible. It moaned as she negotiated more mysterious curves. Before she knew it she was back at the gateway to Baja, at the US border.

"What the …?" wondered Stacy.

"We're in Mexicali!" muttered Arthur, "we're going round in circles, literally" as Arthur looked on the map. She had taken the #5 north. They were now diametrically opposed, equidistant to

Ensenada, where they had originally gone off track.

"Why me, God?" asked Arthur looking skyward. "Go west young woman take the #2. Can you do that?"

Stacy was nearly in tears as she bolted out of town. The lush fertile valleys laiden with wheat, cantelope and cotton, a product of the mighty Colorado River supplying the scorched desert. The spread of the Imperial Valley of California also led to the prosperity of the region.

"No more bull…"stated Arthur as they passed the Plaza de Toros de Califia.

"Si," said Stacy as they raced along the US-Mexican border to Tecate.

"You know where you're driving me?" asked Arthur. "To drink!" he blurted out before she could get a word in edge-wise. He had eyed the Tecate brewery.

"No time for sight seeing" she said defiantly, as she rolled into Tijuana. She had found the passage back to where they had picked up the Mercedes Benz.

"Mama Mia, Santa Maria. Will we ever leave

this place?"

"Yes, I'm always looking out for #1" she joked halfheartedly. Arthur was amused, in fact he broke into a roaring round of laughter. Stacy nearly split her guts as she joined in. After a few minutes of concerted comical hysteria, their tired torsos ached.

"By jove, I think she's got it!" noted Arthur astonished, as he acknowledged the large #1 emblazoned off the Mexican highway.

"See senor, the black tarmac, the #1 down Mexico way?"

"See senorita, you're a genius!" he jested.

The heat waves raged radiating off the black top roadway. Stacy felt like tossing her bikini top, but there were actually other motorists on this stretch. She'd hate to cause a fatal crash, with fortune knocking at her door. Instead, she'd wait for the perfect moment.

Arthur examined the map in the scorching afternoon sun. They were approaching Guerrero Negro, the 'black warrior', named after the old American whaling vessel wrecked in the water near the mouth of the 'Laguna de Ojo de Liebre', one of thousands of lakes in the area.

"It says in the guide, it's the best spot to see the whales make out!" ribbed Arthur.

"No kidding? That must be a sight for sore eyes!" said Stacy.

"It's also one of the world's largest producers of salt. Cedros Island about 55 miles off shore is the shipment transfer stop. Where's my lost shaker of salt?" quipped Arthur as Stacy missed the turnoff to the whale's permiscuous playground.

"The road's up ahead" remarked Arthur. Stacy took a wrong turn onto a deserted bumpy dusty dirt path.

"Some people say that there's a woman to blame" sung the sun struck desperado softly to himself.

The deceptive rays reflected off the shim-mering smooth surface ahead. The water looked so inviting. Stacy stopped the car then leapt out the door.

"Catch me if you can" she shouted as she ran to the elusive watery illusion's edge. Arthur rubbed his eyes as he stepped out of the car. He caught a glimpse of a mirage? Stacy unsnapped her top and flung it afar, then wiggled out of her bikini bottom and kicked it aside. Arthur eyed her wobbling backside as she disappeared in the distance. He was in hot pursuit, trying to unbutton his tropical shirt with one arm. He lost his balance due to the lop sided bouncing cast and bottle of tequila in the other, then keeled over like a drunken sailor in paradise.

"Wait for me!" he pleaded. Stacy was perplexed standing with her hands on her bare hips in the middle of the salt flats. Not a drop of water anywhere in site. "Where's the beach?" she wondered. Arthur soon realized their predicament, the scorching heat had baked the water from the ponds leaving them high and dry, caked in the crusty pure white salt.

"No matter" as her caught a glimpse of her pretty posterior. "Stacy, why don't you just roll around like a beached whale, and I'll lick the salt…" She must've heard him for she soon stormed in his direction.

"Who are you calling a beached whale?" she demanded, standing above him unaware she wasn't wearing a thread. Straddling him like the Colossus of Rhodes, Arthur simply held the bottle up between her legs and squeaked,

"Tequila?"

"Well, I'm waiting!" she fumed.

"You're the most stunning mermaid ever to grace the waters of Mexico" amazed by her curvaceous tanned torso.

"I'll bet you say that to all the women!" rifled Stacy.

"Aren't you forgetting some-thing?"

"What?"

"North and south of the border" he tried to clue her in on her nakedness. She cringed, trying to cover up strategic spots with the palms of her hands. She scrambled to find her things strewn somewhere up ahead.

Arthur returned to the lop sided Mercedes, the rear right tire was flat. He leaned over and spotted the tiny hook embedded in the worn tread.

"Que pasa? I guess I'm not the only lost angler out here looking for nothing."

"Help me find my things!" fumed Stacy frantically trying to retrace her steps as she hopped over the scorching sand. Arthur suddenly noticed a cloud of salty dust stretching across the horizon from the lake bed in the distance. "The Mexican cavalry? Now I know what Davy Crockett felt like at the Alamo as Santa Ana's men marched on the tiny mission." The mechanized Mexican motorcade neared. The roaring revving engines of countless off road raging vehicles was about to engulf them.

"Look over there" shouted Arthur pointing at Stacy.

"Where? I've looked over there."

"No, Look…out!" She continued to hop and shake all about.

"Holy enchilada, do you see what I see, Bob?"

"I should have brought my trusty hunting rifle, I don't believe I've ever seen a Mexican Jack Rabbit that big!"

"Shall we run it down?"

"I'm sure the sight of the Baja war wagons will scare it to death. It might be good eatin' around the campfire after the race?"

Stacy finally found her two piece bikini suit. It was then that she heard the roarin' thunder. She turned around and dropped her things as several vehicles screamed by on either side of her.

"What the…?"

"And uh, they're off!"

"Let the best man win!"

"Is that any way to start a race?" questioned the curious two man crews, as they veered and spun out on the salty flats. A massive traffic jam ensued. Stacy simply buried her face in her hands.

"Some people say that there's a woman to blame…" repeated Arthur endlessly like a broken record.

At least she had 'flagged down' some desperately needed help. If left on their own, the vultures and buzzards might be the only spectators coming to watch.

15: Won't Get Fooled Again!

"Love is as much an object as an obsession, everybody wants it, everybody seeks it, but few ever achieve it, those who do will cherish it, be lost in it, and among all will never …never forget it."
- Curtis Judalet

Stacy slipped into her skimpy yet more modest racing gear. She had turned a shade of rock lobster red from embarrassment and the Mexican rays.

"Well little lady" stated a dusty bandana draped desperado, "What seems to be the problem?" he asked sarcastically as he noticed her plentiful package.

"I presume, you and your boy-friend are in one heck of a pickle" he predicted as he eyed the immobilized Mercedes, the character in his confining cast, and his cute albeit clumsy co-pilot. What a curious duo of desperados.

"You got that right, we just seem to be going in circles spinning our wheels, so to speak."

"I can see that." The rest of the energized entourage found the pair quite amusing.

"No kidding, my side kick, Stacy has come full circle from Ensenanda, via San Felipe, Mexicali, Tijuana and back."

"Well, you two aren't unlike the rest of us. The teams competing on the 1000 km circuit from Ensenada to La Paz and back, slightly bigger circuit, bigger wheels. But you have us beat in one department. Baja or Bust"

"Can you help us? Can we buy one of your buggies? I'll offer you anything? The sky's the limit."

"Are you pulling my leg?" asked an oily parched person, probably from the pit crew.

"No, he's not kidding" snapped Stacy defending the busker. "He's incognito, down here, scouting a location for an upcoming production" she said boldly.

"Where's your chopper?"

"It's in service in LA or San Diego"

"Sure, and I'm the president of Mexico on a joy ride."

"Please to meet you" said Arthur, "Should I make out the cheque to you personally or the entire country?"

"Ha, ha, …..he ain't kidding?"

"No, we're here on business" continued Stacy in his defense.

"Are you some kind of celebrity, busker? A comedian, a street performer. It's how many a star got their start in Hollywood.

"Who do you think I am?"

"I can't place the face. Bob Hope, George Burns, Robin Williams began as buskers burnishing, polishing their acts to the countless crowds."

"Hmmmm" he had heard of famous personalities disguising them-selves to remain anonymous from all the unwanted admirers.

"It also applies to singers, Paul McCartney, Sting, Rod Stewart, Bob Dylan, even Bon Jovi, ……you vaguely resemble Dolly Parton, miss, she was a busker."

"A busker or bust…er."

"Watch it buster."

"Sorry, but I've had more than my fair share of female sight seeing today" said Arthur apologetically.

"Well I'd give my left nut to have such a cute co-pilot" to cruise through the barren countryside.

"You can have her, she couldn't navigate her way out of the open broad-side door of a barn!" rebutted Arthur.

"Are you implying I'm a country bumpkin? Arthur."

"Hand picked, country grown…"

"I'd quit while you were ahead."

"I'd listen to the little lady, or she'll have your head on a platter! There's nothing worse than a woman scorned."

"She's all yours, she's only a loaner!"

"I'd never feel alone again with you by my side ma'am."

"Thanks, but I think he means I am his private nurse, from a complying colleague of his. I'm only here to get him from point A to B."

"Baja or Bust? We noticed the plates.

"You can't even get your bear…rings….."

"I like what I've seen so far."

"But I wouldn't want to impose, be –sides, your tractor needs more than a tune up I reckon. Neither one of those snazzy foreign imports nor a John Deere are any match for this Mexican wasteland."

"We rely on the latest technology and modified buggies to get us around the Mexican merry go round trip from Ensenada to La Paz in about a week."

"Bull…."

"No sir. We have the most sophisticated satellite tracking system, the Pentagon's GPS Washington's COMSAT via Inmarsat transmitting up to the minute data from the engine to our tracking station in Cerro de Borrego, Mexico"

"No way?" wondered Stacy.

"Yes, we have up to the minute status reports displayed every 15 minutes to monitor vital engine components. The tracking vehicles can retrace our tracks and recover a downed dune buggy. A quick pit stop and we're good to go!"

"My God, it's a miracle! I thought you were

simply a mirage."

"One mirage you don't want to be without out here."

"Well then I'll take a his and hers model for me and the misses" joked Arthur.

"Sorry, no can do! We could possibly part with one vehicle, the 'Lone Ranger' if the price were right, but who's going to drive the mega horse power monster?"

"You're right. Stacy could never tame this beast."

"Watch me!" she dared.

"I've seen quite enough" Arthur paused for a few moments. Stacy pleaded and applied her persuasive charming duality.

"Pretty please" she purred in his ear. I'll make it up to you."

"Sold to the sexy senorita with the smile." She kissed Arthur, her tongue spread his lips, her tongue reached down his throat.

"Leapin' lizards lady, save your appetite for the luau. That is if we ever get there."

"Thanks Arthur my sweet guacamole pie, you're the greatest."

"Ah shucks" squirmed the other racing crew. "pitter patter, let's get at her. John, could you show Stacy how to shift."

"Shift?"

"Good God! I'm sure my Lear could land on these salt flats, but I'm sworn to silence. This is one picture I'm going to produce on my own!"

"They don't come in automatic?"

"Takes all the fun out of the frenzied furious pace. You'll want to feel every bump and curve in the road."

"Ease her in gently, gringo!" insisted Arthur.

"I'm no spring chicken."

"Or stranger to danger" added Arthur surprised by her drive and determination to conquer this set back. She may have tipped the scales in her favor to land a lead role in the film. If only he could now get his act together and rally the troops and piece the plot together. It was in the palm of his hands, the dynamite winner had not donned upon him yet. He had to rely on her impulsive instincts, she on his. Somehow the two buskers (Spanish –to seek) would find what they were looking for.

"Seek and ye shall find" stated John as Stacy fretted as she found first gear. She tried to synchronize her foot and hand movements, no more difficult than chewing gum and walking at the same time she figured. The Lone Ranger kicked up a stream of salty white powder and lurched forward. She spun the vehicle, nearly lapsing into vertigo simply to test the traction. The tires bit the salty surface, the wounds ran deep as she revved the engine, lost between first and second. She rounded a circular course the crew had set up with the other dune buggies. Stacy eyed the third vehicle and slammed it into third gear. The team ducked as she seasoned them with the salty spray.

"This is the perfect place to practice" she expelled, excited by her first go-round. Certainly not the standard scenario for a prospective employer. This extracurricular activity was downright exhilirating. It gave a boost to her confidence. Arthur was simply a puppet missing out on all the action. At least with his fortune he could pay for any frivolous form of transport-ation he desired. This would do in a pinch! Such divine intervention" mused Stacy.

"I think you've got the hang of it, yeah I think you're good" said John astounded by her aptitude.

"Why don't you follow us at least for the first few miles, after that you're on your own."

"Sure." The posse mounted their speedy souped up steeds.

"We'll call for reinforcements to pick up the Mercedes and tow it to Cabos, that was where you were heading?"

"Si."

"There's plenty here for the trip. Thanks again Arthur, I hope you two have a great honeymoon!"

"Don't mention it, keep the tip!" Tip? He figured he was given enough to furnish an entire fleet of free wheeling wagons for future races.

Arthur couldn't resist, and gave the charge salute, "High ho silver, away," as his snoopy goggles and scarf fluttered in the sweltering afternoon air. Not fit for man nor beast, a siesta under a shady tree limb the preferred practice in these parts. The formation formed a single line with the lead vehicle vanishing in the sinking sun slightly above the horizon. Stacy and Arthur left the prowling pack to fend for themselves, to resume their annual ritual. Conquering the rugged course rounding near the tip of Baja then rebound back to Ensenada. The arduous highly taxing trek, a testimony to teamwork, well tuned machines and minds of steel. It may trickle over to prepare the pair for the Bisbee's competition. Their main adversary, the elusive fish. But with the modern sonar, the slippery specimens of the deep were as good as dead in the water!

They continued to trail the pack, lagging further behind. The GPS systems would not let them out of their sights. The main cluster moved steadily toward the target, the turning point in LaPaz. The solitary shining star had come to rest at a blackened sandy beach of Mulege, another oasis in the middle of the menacing Mexican desert. Stacy hydroplaned across the gentle surf as it lapped onto the shore. She turned the key in the ignition, her motor was still revving, running hot. She peeled off her parched two piece suit and rushed to the water's edge to prevent her radiator from over heating. Arthur stirred snug as a bug in a rug strapped into the Recarro racing seat. He could see from 'Here to Eternity'. Images of the romantic tryst saturated his mind. The memorable embrace on the beach by Burt Lancaster and Deborrah Kerr back in 1953 confused him. Oh how he longed to recreate that moment with his mistress. In his condition the performance would be a shoe in, equally arousing as the winner of 8 Academy Awards, including Best Picture, Best Supporting Actor and Actress, Cinematography and Directing. The challenge was to perform all functions with one additional handicap, the hot husky cast like a giant ear of corn concealing his appendage.

"Come on in, the water's lovely Arthur" encouraged Stacy frolicking in the foamy spray. He eased himself out of the dune buggy and discovered his sunburnt dilemma. He side stepped to the water's edge like a forlorn fiddler crab looking for his female fiddling companion.

"This isn't going to be easy" said Arthur assessing the acrobatics involved in the maneuver. "Stacy"

"Arthur, come on in!"

"But my cast!"

"A little water isn't going to kill you, besides, don't you want me?"

"Indeed I do!"

He wobbled up to the receding surf, the cool California current licked his toes. He waited for the right moment, then leapt forward. He slipped and struck his head and was sucked under in the tow. Stacy sprung into action, hauling the hulk out of danger and dragged him onto shore then rolled on top and pinned his cast. She pinched his nose and expelled her large tidal volume of air into Arthur. He choked and coughed up some seaweed finally astir. Her haunting hazel eyes, glowing bright orbs custom designed in heaven he figured. Stacy kissed him for what seemed like a lifetime. He'd soon have to come up for air ere she'd have to throw him a lifeline. Arthur wrapped his tiny free arm around her like a feisty fidler crab.

"Now that's a wrap!" he said

"Close your eyes don't peek!"

He complied. She scooped up her string bikini, tied a tight knot then hopped into the buggy. She slid into her slinky taut white jumpsuit which had shrunk a size in the sizzling sunlight; then cranked the key into the ignition and fired up the beast. The roar startled the prostrate performer.

"Come on lover, you've got my motor runnin'."

Arthur proud of his prowess leapt to his feet as Stacy lurched ahead.

"Catch me if you can!" she taunted him always a few feet ahead.

"Touche, you win, I'm eternally indebted to you."

"And?"

"And I'll make you a big star. You'll be in the movies."

"Marvelous", she mimicked any number of memorable motion picture stars Arthur knew a winner when he saw one. They whistled down the highway and ventured along the seaside boulevard. The natives were restless as the steady Latin beat grew. They lovebirds left the buggy outside the Xstasis, themselves both in a state of ecstasy. The laser beams bounced off their brilliant radiating smiles, nearly blinding the bouncers in the process. Stacy's body hugging suit was an eye popper, a show stopper, while Arthur completed the curious couple with his massive cast. As if going to their first gala performance, intent on taking home the prize, their own Academy Award. Their dream was suddenly shattered as gunfire ricocheted out side. A few bouncers dash-ed outside to see what all the commotion was about.

"Just another damn dune buggy!" he said.

Stacy and Arthur rushed to the entrance, pushing their way through the mob.

"Looks like the lone ranger rides again!" he said sadly as their wheels vanished in the sunset.

16: Mock Hotel California

"Mirrors on the ceiling, the pink
champagne on ice..."
-Don Henley, lyrics from
the best selling song

The pink petal to the metal sailed along the Mexican highway as a breath of fresh air, a rose among the thorny thistles and tumble weeds of the desolate terrain. She was thinking to herself this could be heaven, or this could be hell. They thought they'd never find sanctuary or a safe harbor and simply sail off the face of the at land's end. Cali and the Cadillac Crooners saw a shimmering light up ahead in the distance, then heard the mission bell. An oasis or a mirage in the middle of nowhere? A sign? 'Hotel California' slapped onto the side of the Mediterranean façade, startled them. Such a lovely face such a lovely place. They're living' it up at.... ......the lyrics lingered in her mind. They had to get a room for the night, to rest their weary bones. To ease their minds Cali was heart broken. Pedro was married to his bulls, a pretty senorita simply a distraction. His true love, the bloody thrust of his saber, the destruction of a defenseless creature. How could her Don Juan be cap-able of loving anything but himself any-way? If he inconceivably left his guard down, he'd fall prey to his formidable opponent. Death always knocking at his door! "To hell with you Pedro" she fumed. The Cadillac crooners sensed her edginess They tried in vain to comfort, console her

"Bottle those morose memories; save 'em, savor them, let it simmer in that surprisingly creative stew up there" stated John tapping her forehead. "We have a show tomorrow night. You can let the genie out of the bottle then!"

"That's brilliant" said Steve.

"Yeah, channel your frustration and energy and simply knock 'em dead. Project your passion play for all to see. You know how charged your performances can be. They're simply electric. Even the night man felt the tension of the band members.

"Plenty of room at the Hotel California, relax" said the night man, "we are programmed to receive. You can check out anytime you like……"

It reminded Cali of another chapter in her life, so long ago. She had wanted to bury the past, but it kept resurfacing, auto rewind, over and over again. The dreamy diorama unfolded as soon as they walked through the doors. Perhaps truly an inspirational place to spur on her overactive imagination or insane asylum, the multicolored palette of pretty colors changed at every corner like her mixed up mind. Was she truly a part of this success story waiting to be written or were they just more of the pretty, pretty boys that she called friends? The staff followed them through the courtyard, hauling their heavy equipment. They sweat profusely, but the fragrant floral collection in full bloom masked the odor. They caught a glimpse of the Coronela Bar, barely big enough to host a solo Spanish guitarist, let alone their gig.

"Most of the 'big buskers at one time or another came through these narrow hallowed halls here in Todos Santos. (All Saints in spanish) Almost all went on to greener pastures to find their fame and fortune. I wouldn't sweat it" said the bartender.

"It's perfect, I'm getting a few vibes, good, good, good good vibrations" Cali began to twirl about the quaint cozy corridors osmosing the magic.

"It's like she's so in tune with life" marveled Steve. "I don't know how she does it? After all she's been through, the deadly encounters with drugs, the hallucinations. She's like Keith Richards, just oozing, dripping with ….emotion."

"Exactly, we have to find a way to tap her energy, there are so many experiences lurking in the recesses of her mind…"

"What's on tap?"

"Try me" tempted the astute bartender.

"Bohemia, Corona, Estrella, Modelo, Modelo Especial, Negro Modelo and Pacifico, do I pass miss?"

"Cali, Cali Columbia" The bartender felt she was fabricating the name, perhaps a peculiar stage presence. She didn't seem to fit the bill, but decided to play along.

"OK Cal, can I call you that?"

"You can call me anything you like…"

"Willy Velaquez."

"Well Willy Vee, let's see what you've got, surprise me."

"Cucapa? It's on tap and it's cold."

"Cucapa, any relation to the five tribes living in Mexicali?"

"Bingo, the original settlers of the region, noted for their love of nature and water. They later moved to the Colorado River delta."

"Magnificent, free Willy?"

"Sure, this microbrew's on me."

"I'll have a Munchner Negro Modelo" said Steve trying to lighten their lagging spirit.

"I'll have a Corona" said John.

"It's company we all plan to be in some day."

"How so?"

"The American style lager is the number one import beer in the world. If only we could latch our label and CD's onto each bottle."

"Cali and the Cadillac Crooners has kind of a swingin' 60's ring to it like the Beach Boys, Eagles, Van Halen, by the look of your list. Who knows, it might catch on? You're booked into the Cabo Wabo this weekend aren't you?"

"Yeah."

"Sammy Hagar's legendary rockin' club's been a winner from the get go! It's a crucial gauge, a steppin' stone for the great ones."

"Yeah, it gives me the willy's."

"No offense."

"None taken."

"Just act natural. Whale out those wonderful tunes. Belt out a boomin' bass beat and you'll reel in the whole town."

"We'll turn it down, here, a tad. Was that the holy Todos Santos (Sp.- All Saints) choir I heard in neighboring church as we came in?"

"You're right on the money. I can ask a few of them to accompany you if you like. Perhaps get down and dirty with some devilish lyrics. You've got all day. Use the Hotel to test the waters, a testing ground, a testament of your musical talent."

"We'll give it some thought, pen a few bars, let the saints march in and in-spire us. We're bound to synthesize a spellbinding stage presence" said Cali formulating a few concepts as they spoke.

"Sounds a little spooky if you ask me" said Steve as he waved his fingers in front of her face."

The glitzy golden skull ring on his forefinger reflected and caught the eye of an enchanting enchilada entering the far end of the bar.

"Clara is that you?" The senorita looked confused, gaunt, bony, as if on her last legs. Willy offered her a tequila shot glass. She crept up to the end of the dark alabaster bar. Her bony digits dug through the bowl of limes, as if clawing out of a coffin, incoherently. She was severely dehydrated.

"Muerte (sp.– death)" said Cali as she reached over to feel her forehead. The woman was oblivious to her advance. Her skin was cold and clammy "She's deathly ill, and needs a doctor…"

"Or an undertaker?" wondered Willy.

"What's wrong with her?" asked Steve as he covered the skull with his hands. The skull and crossbones came to Cali's mind, the inscription on a bottle of poison. She had had so many near death experiences, herself, she was nearly a living legend, a testimony to life after death. She looked deeply into the wasting woman's widely dilated pupils, then offered to hold her lifeless hands. Her pulse was weak and rapid. She was shaking uncontrollably, Cali tried to warm her by rubbing her arms.

"Has she seen a ghost?"

Clara was thoroughly confused. She bit into every lime but spit them out.

"She's OD ing on cocaine salts, she has no sense of taste and smell, lack of hunger. Her throat's probably burning.

"Shouldn't we call a doctor?"

"There's no time, we have to act fast. Do you have any tea bags and hot water?"

"Yeah, sure thing."

"Cocaine Cali?"

"She must've just injected. If we can induce vomiting…"

"The tannic acid in a strong steeped tea."

"Clara, can you hear me?" Cali searched her arms but found no needle marks. Odd. Did you inhale?"

"There are no sign of cocaine salts in her nostrils nor bloody moth eaten nasal passages."

Clara slumped over and slipped into a coma. She died shortly thereafter and fell off her barstool. The fall would have killed her. Cali picked up the petite wasted woman.

"We were too late!"

"We're always too late!" fumed Willy.

"What do you mean?"

"We've had an epidemic in these parts. The hookers, the prostitutes the women of the night. Every so often one will drop like a fly."

"Oh?"

"They usually come in here then go to the mission to pray. Like an anointing of last rites, a ritual. They just seem to disappear in the desert, to wander off and die without a trace. Like the song says 'you can check out anytime you like ….."

"But you can never leave?" It brought back nightmares of Camarillo. How many more may have died in the institute by mishandled medications? Was this place a mirror image?

"What do you mean without a trace? There's

always a body."

"Let it go Cali" pleaded the other band members. "Let sleeping dogs lie."

"That's just it, there isn't" said Willy, reeling in his Tony Lama boots

"Well, we have one now."

"I don't think her family would want us to intervene. She was the mayor's daughter. She'll have a traditional burial, let her rest in peace!"

Cali felt she was always partially to blame, her father's long history, his formidable degree of infiltration. The tempting candy always seemed to find its way into every corner store or the most comfortable establishment. It was a priceless form of basic barter, leading to a paperless fortune. She felt divine intervention had led her here, the deadly duality of a diabolical double universe?

"Cali, we'd better get some shut eye" suggested the other spooked buskers. We're on the brink of a break through, a music deal? This is no time for a break-down."

"I feel fine" she insisted, but I'm beginning to worry about you boys, life's a beach ain't it?" she stated. "We've all had a long trying day. I'm just trying to make a little sense out of it."

"Why don't you all sleep on it?" asked Willy. "The drinks were on me."

"No, nothing in life is free Willy, here this ought to cover the tab."

"Gracios. If there's anything the staff or I can get you…."

"A wake up call about 8. We'll take our breakfast by the pool." Steve was beginning to assume the lifestyle of a rock star. The mysterious death simply a prop to promote their peculiar evolving style. All the greats were after all a product of their own unique experiences. A repertoire of tunes, a reflection of the times. Their gig, a mock up adaptable to any venue.

"I suppose you'll have the 'mock pink champagne on ice' with your breakfast?"

"A mock ….?"

"1/2 cup sugar, 1 ½ cups water, ½ cup orange juice, 2 cups cranberry juice, 1 cup pineapple juice, and 2 bottles lemon lime soda."

"But there's no champagne."

"You can thank me later, a little preventative medicine, er detox never hurt anyone."

"I think I'd rather have the house special, the Mission Bell isn't it? A large fish bowl or punch bowl will do. Plenty of ice, squeeze one lemon 'til the juice runs down my leg', add two 750 ml bottles of white dinner wine, 12 oz of brandy, and 16 oz of orange juice, no pulp, stir well, when we're all seated add the champagne, stirring gently garnish the glasses with orange slices."

"That serves about 30."

"Invite the staff, it's a breakfast of champions. It's good to start your day with a bang, that amount of alcohol will alleviate any angst, likely induce a good hearty laugh. Laughter is the best medicine after all."

"I'll prepare the potion myself" stated Willy the wily coyote.

"It'll give the festivities a kick start ease the edginess at the funeral, unleash our potential…"

"If you don't pass out by high noon" predicted Cali. "I think I'll pass. Pay my respects to the family, find out a few more facts. Help out in any way I can."

"I just want you to take a little time out to smell the roses, savor the sweet flavor of impending success. You came into our lives out of nowhere, and turned this band upside down. You compli-ment our overall concept. Your musical abilities are only out done by your allure and beauty."

"Oh, please, don't patronize me!"

"We're simply paying you the respect, you so desperately deserve."

"You're a tough nut to crack, Cali."

"You're part of our musical family now. The missing piece in the jigsaw puzzle jingle."

"OK."

"I'm flattered, but part of me is still a free bird, I can't be caged or fenced in by anyone."

"Well we're not here to stifle your creativity, but broaden your horizons, bring out your full potential."

"I don't need a sermon from the mount" she insisted. "That I can get from our father in the church. Your lecture has a curious anaesthetic quality about it though. I'm sure you mean well. I still have unresolved issues to address."

17: Cali Columbia

"Freedom has it's life in the hearts, the actions, the spirit of men and so it must be daily earned and refreshed – else like a flower cut from it's life giving roots, will wither and die"
- Dwight D. Eisenhower

Cali was awoken by the cock's crow at the crack of dawn. The first rays of light had crept into her bedroom and cast an eerie blood red glow on the bull's skull hanging from the wall opposite the bed. She marched to the window and parted the shutters and peeked out. The mission bell rang twice, once a high pitch then a low boom. Several people had gathered early, probably the gardeners, she figured, as they snipped the colorful floral plumage in preparation for the funeral. The bright marigolds, the scented herbs of Mexico were meticulously maintained. Some strains lent themselves to horticultural tending. The unique multicolored mane of the cockscomb, or Celasia Cris-tata, looked like a rooster's comb as the name implied. It grew both in the humid and arid regions and was even harvested as food in many parts of South America. The particularly high number of seeds in each flower insured it's survival, upwards of 43,000/ounce. Sometimes called 'pink castle' the red, yellow, orange or pink plumage would be particularly pleasing for the family of the departed. Cali got dressed. Not a soul was stirring in the hotel, so she snuck out and wandered to the small cemetery. The long shadows of the tombstones, as the suns rays gathered, cast a somber ambience over the grounds. A few early risers had gathered a few buckets and placed them on the grave-sites.

"It's so peaceful at this time" she said trying to strike up a conversation.

"Si senorita" said the elderly woman. She stared

at Cali for an eternity.

"You remind me of my own daughter. She passed away a few days ago."

"I'm sorry."

"Gracios."

"What are you doing?"

"I'm preparing for the offerings, the adornment of the admirers, paying their respects."

"Bouquets?"

"Too numerous to count."

"It's part of our Hispanic Roman Catholic custom, isn't it? From what little I remember from my father, mostly old family photographs."

"Yes, for the entire month of October and November, the 'Dia de Muertos', the 'Day of the Dead'."

"It's that time of year again" said Cali comically, almost coldly.

"Si, it should be a festive time!"

"The music and merriment; we seem to be among the very few people who live it up at such a normally somber occasion."

"Strange isn't it?"

"How so?"

"For many who lived such sad, morbid, lonely lives, alienated from their families, their deaths bring such joy to their loved ones." She was speaking more from her own morose experiences.

"Si, but all saints will come marching home on all saints day, next month." The old woman placed a few papel picado or paper mache cutouts along with a few silk stemmed flowers on top of the mound. When the funeral procession passes by later today, they'll place the freshly cut plants into the buckets. You can come if you like."

"Gracios, but I always cry at funerals."

"Oh, I think you'll enjoy yourself."

"How so?"

"Once you hear the merry mariachi's tunes you'll have a change of heart. Upwards of nine band members may perform."

"You're kidding?"

"One of two trumpets, up to four saxophones, two drummers and maybe even a tuba if we're lucky and he hasn't had too many tequilas the night before."

"I'll think about it."

"Oh do come, if only for the food."

"Food?"

"All the fresh baked goods and delicious treats for the dearly departed. It is placed on the grave sites or even tables set up. The spirits need it for their journey."

"Journey?"

"To pay us a holiday visit." Cali wondered about the old woman.

"Si, senorita, that's my girl. We haven't had that spirit here since 1969."

"Excuse me?" Perhaps her tired mind was playing tricks on her.

"I didn't say anything" said the gardener. "But can you help me arrange these candles, and copal."

"Incense?"

"Yes, and later, fireworks."

Cali stood up and brushed the soil from her knees. It was refreshing to tend to a tiny plot. A young woman came and stood beside her. She had a forlorn look on her pretty face.

"The band will cheer you up" said Cali, the old woman insured me. She…"

"What old woman?"

"She was right here, I was talking to her."

"I heard you speak those heart warming words. She pulled a photo from her pocket."

"Your family?"

"Si, they're back in Columbia. I'm Consuela."

"From which part? My father was from Columbia. I'm Cali from California."

"Buenaventura."

"Good fortune. It means good fortune in Spanish."

"I know what it means. It's meaningless. A sweltering humid haven of homicide, that's what it is. 300,000 people on devil's island (Cascajal) the size of of LA, with 24 X the murder rate of New York."

"But it's the main pacific port, for a thriving export business for gold, platinum, bananas...."

"It's a living hell. Over 300,000 people have fled to neighboring states and regions, those lucky enough to escape."

"Why?"

"Archangel Henao, the drug lord, the devil himself is trying to take over the entire port."

"My family paid for my plastic surgery, a passport to the promised land and prosperity they told me. So many other women would sell their souls to escape. To come to California."

"Liberty: One of imagination's most precious possessions." (Ambrose Bierce, The Devil's Dictionary).

"Their surgeons were students of Dr Pitanguy, but who knows who they are really working for."

"What do you mean?"

"Haven't you heard?"

"The Cali Cartel was busted."

"What?"

"The two brothers, the big fish were caught."

"Rodriguez? I had heard of them, but…."

"Si, Gilbert Rodriguez Orejuela, 'the chess player', the mastermind behind the biggest cartel since the Columbian police killed Escobar in 1993. His brother Miguel 'el senor' is next. To be deported to Miami from what I've heard from the other women."

"Other women?"

"They're constantly arriving in the arid desert resort towns, bound for California, usually LA."

"Like yourself?"

"Si, I've been waiting in limbo for the past

five years waiting for my ride."

"Your ride?"

"We were all guaranteed safe passage to southern California, but most of us never make it. We are dropped off, destined for our exotic locations."

"Now you've nearly taken root here?"

"Yes, many beautiful women wander the streets looking for work. In time they become the working girls of the street, the concubines catering to the wealthy tourists. Their holiday just beginning. Our journey usually coming to a tragic end. The few that have struggled to escape mysteriously disappear without a trace. No bodies have been found."

"And the drug lords?"

"Rodriguez's assets, close to $2.1 billion attained from 1990-2002 were seized. They built their empires on the backs of the mules exporting their exotic enticing drug. We were all caught up in his network. $7 billion a year supplying 80% of the world's cocaine."

"Doesn't most of it go up to the United States though?"

"They are their own worst enemies. They

consume the lion's share. Columbia produces 430 metric tones of cocaine, the world's largest supplier on greater than 114,000 hectares of cultivated land. Another 2100 hectares are devoted to heroin, 3.8 metric tones of pure heroin."

"All bound for the US?"

"Si."

"But, we have an effective anti narcotics plan, the president has committed more than $1.3 billion to halt the production."

"It is a drop in the bucket compared to the fierce Fortune 500 run cartels. They are the envy of the entire export industry."

"But most of the crops have been grazed, no?"

"No! aerial spraying measures have eradicated some 130,000 hectares of coca, but the aggressive replantation process is highly organized. The cartels launder money in all forms, shapes and sizes in black market pesos. 300 'baby cartels' have sprung up in Columbia alone. To compound the problem, newer hardier strains of cocaine are emerging."

"Like our MRSA infections?" (Methicillin Resistant Staph Aureus)

"Yes, rumor has it there is a RRC strain"

"RRC?"

"Roundup Ready Cocaine strain. Do you recall in 1996 Monsanto was experimenting with a roundup ready soybean impervious to glyophosate, a deadly fumigant?"

"Vaguely, I believe my father was a pioneer in protecting his crops."

"Well rumor has it that a resistant strain of cocaine has emerged. Invincible even to Fusarium the strongest cidal agent."

"It's a never ending battle."

"A deadly circle, a perpetual cycle. The cartels spend millions to train their engineers and chemists in the best US universities who in turn return to perfect the formula and Fortune 500 networks."

"But why doesn't the US simply say NO, and stop importing?"

"Can one stop the rain? The North Valley cartel is practically invincible. They use submarines, rumor has it a Russian sub purchased by a Cali cartel sunk off the pacific coast because they had no crew to operate it."

"No kidding?"

"Sophisticated programs with encryption methods to know when satellites and P3 Orion surveillance craft are coming. They simply wait it out or redistribute their cargos. They have even resorted to developing a plastic cocaine which can be embedded in fish tanks and any other form of export."

"They're unstoppable."

"May be, May be not? But word has it among the women, they are onto something?"

"A link in the chain of command."

"Oh?"

"A few of the cabin cruisers are frequenting more of our favorite fishing spots."

"For business or pleasure?"

"Who knows? perhaps their business is pleasure or visa versa?"

"What I'm saying is, they may be setting up strategic linkages in newer businesses. In the early days it was gambling, casinos, now it may be the film industry for all I know?"

"Redistribute their wealth?"

"Star bartering power. They sold us on the

dream. Nothing more than a sick sentence into exile. I fear I'll never leave this place alive!"

"Your strong faith has kept you whole. There's always a ray of hope over the horizon. Hang onto it. It's the only way I've survived."

"Gracios ..?"

"Cali, Cali Columbia. Why don't you come to the Hotel tonight. We're playing at the 'Hotel California'. Show starts at sunset."

The chatty Chiquita's conversation ceased abruptly as if she'd seen a ghost busker.

"I'll be there."

"Bring as many guests as you like, some of the other desperate women, dance to the beat of a different drum. They wish they all could be California girls don't they?"

"I suppose, we all have to keep our dreams alive."

Cali longed for the water again, her little isolated island of Avalon, untainted by the trafficker's terrorism. Her Isla Bonita. The Hotel pool had to suffice as she strolled into the patio. The pink champagne glasses were strewn over the tables the orange and lime rinds were piled on the plates pell mell, helter skelter. She peeled off her t shirt and dove into the warm water and let it embrace her entire body. A cleansing ritual, to revive herself. Give it time to stir the melodies lingering in her mind as the afternoon disappeared.

"There she is, we've been looking all over town for you. Come on, Cali we have a show in a half hour."

Willy, the spirited emcee introduced the new Mexican minstrels, Cali and the Cadillac Crooners. The lights dimmed as the tiny ensemble began to enchant the handful of sexy enchiladas who had parked themselves in every available seat in the house. "On a dark desert highway cool wind in my hair" began the band "warm smell of colitis rising up through the air. Up ahead in the distance I saw a shimmering light, my head grew heavy, my sight grew dim, I had to stop for the night. There she stood in the doorway,…" Consuela peeked around the corner then ventured into the lounge, with all but the band in complete silence. The room was aglow in hundreds of lit candles, a debt to the dead. "I heard the mission bell, and I was thinking to myself this could be heaven or this could be hell.

Then she lit up a candle and she showed me the way. There were voices in the corridor, I thought I heard them say." The band encouraged everyone to join in, even the choir…:"Welcome to the Hotel California, such a lovely place, such a lovely face. Plenty of room at the Hotel California, any time of year you can find it here." The choir ceased their chant Cali stepped forward with a solo as she stared at each face in the crowd…."Her mind is tiffany twisted, she's got the mercedes bends, she got a lot of pretty pretty boys that she calls friends. How they dance in the courtyard, sweet summer sweat, some dance to remember, some dance to forget. So I called up the captain, please bring me some wine. He said we haven't had that spirit here since 1969. The choir joined in once again "And still those voices were calling from far away, wake you up in the middle of the night just to hear them say…..Welcome to the hotel California such a lovely place such a lovely face, They livin' it up at the hotel California, What a nice surprise bring your alibis." Cali continued her séance like solo as if summoning a lost soul from some-where else. "Mirrors on the ceiling, the pink champagne on ice, And she said we are all just prisoners here of our own device. And in the master's chambers, they gathered for the feast, they stab it with their steely knives but they just can't kill the beast." Her mind conjured up the images of the cartel's cruel bloody war. "Last thing I remember I was running for the door, I had to find the passage back to the place I was before. Relax said the night man we are programmed to receive. You can check out any time you like but you can never leave." The lyrics upset Consuela. She began to cry storming for the exit.

"Consuela wait" shouted Cali as she set the microphone down on her stool.

18: Hukilau

Ancient Hawaiian fishing method.
Lau- leaves, attached to ropes to scare the fish into nets which are then pulled (huki) onto the beach usually by the entire community

The pretty people left their collection of fine cars lined along the marina. The countless yachts and cabin cruisers were comfortably anchored and corralled in the tiny harbor. The bright lights of the lighthouse lured them in as the sun set in Cabos San Lucas. The opening night for the gala regatta and good will fishing fortunes was launched from the legendary club at land's end on the Baja strip.

The entire town converged on the 'Cabo Wabo' as if riding in on a magical wave. Many seasoned anglers and their teams had come from all four corners of the globe to attend an angler's dream. The local Mexican crews were sure that San Lucas, the patron Saint Luke would bless them with a bountiful catch. In any event the indigenous invigorated inhabitants were set for another record breaking reel- in. The rockin' rollin' festival was soon in full swing, in high gear as the tequila gold flowed like water. The men were ready to shake their rods, the women were sexier and slipperier than the smoothest sailfish. Sammy Hagar, the host and proud owner, stepped up to the microphone,

"Thanks for comin' out folks, guys, dolls, anglers, angels, pretty maids all in a row. You've made this the biggest and best event in Cabo. I know we're all ultimately here for one simple reason. To reel in the really big one, the catch of the day. To get our motors runnin' and off to a roarin' start, I'd like to welcome a tasty treat to the club. The gal and her guys, the guys and their doll, or the girl and her beach boys, I give you 'Cali and the Cadillac Crooners'". The audience whet their whistles and gave a rousing round of applause. The band dressed in beach wear, Cali in a shimmering grass skirt shook the crowd. They began with a slightly revised rendition of 'California Girls', "Well east coast girls are hip, I really dig those styles they wear And the southern girls with the way they talk, They knock me out when I'm down there, The mid west farmer's daughters Really make you feel alright, and the northern girls with the way they kiss, They keep their boyfriends warm at night, The west coast has the sunshine and the girls all get so tanned…"

"Yeah, miss Hawaiian tropic."

"I dig a French bikini on a Hawaiian island, Dolls by a palm tree in the sand. I been all around this great big world, And I seen all kinds of girls, but I couldn't wait to get back to Baja to see the cutest girls in the world. I wish they all could be Cabo Wabo girls, I wish they all could be Cabo Wabo girls, I wish they all could be Cabo Wabo girls…"

"That's it Stacy" slobbered Arthur "wiggle your wangos". The two were bounced around the dance floor like everyone else in a giant pin ball arcade.

Consuela was thoroughly confused after only a few tequila shooters but shook her booty with the best of them. Dr Gum was gyrating surrounded by several hula hooped hotties as they wiggled their hips. The dance floor was rockin' flooded full of Wabos, all weebblin', no one had fallen yet. Ere anyone found their seats, the band bounced into another beach Boys tune, "Well I'm not braggin' babe so don't put me down, But I've got the fastest set of wheels in town, When something comes up to me he don't even try Cause if I had a set of wings I know she could fly, She's my little deuce coupe, You don't know what I've got, my little deuce coupe, you don't know what I've got….."

"What's the matter?" yelled Stacy amongst the swingers and swayers. Arthur's grimace had suddenly changed, as if he'd swallowed an entire lemon.

"The Lone Ranger, our little deuce coupe. It's all my fault."

"Don't worry, be happy, it's only a dune buggy, let them have it, you can always buy another one."

"I guess you're right!" A giant grin burst onto his face "Rock on!" ranted Arthur. The band shifted gears once again with another modified melody: 'In My Cabin Cruiser' (Car) "When I'm behind the wheel, horses of gas and steel, The ocean (highway) is my home, in fiberglass and chrome, Fantasy cruiser (car) shiny C & C (corvette), Let's take a ride you can't forget, Come on pretty lady ride with me......."I'm master of my fate when I accelerate, my new C & C (vette) is my throne when on the sea (road) we roam we roam we roam, Cruisin' like we're in a dream, feelin' like we're still sixteen, being a part of the great American scene..."

The pretty playmates propositioned Dr Gum to take them on an unforgettable midnight cruise later. Consuela brought a big banana plantation owner to her table, while Stacy staid with her not so stable first mate, Arthur.

"In my C&C (car) I'm captain of my destiny, in my C & C pretty babe come cruise with me....in my C & C (car) I'm captain of my destiny, in my C & C pretty babe come cruise with me..."

The advanced and amateur anglers, auto afficionados and nacho munchin motorheads lapped up the lyrics and their mouth watering marguerites.

"Let's have some fun, fun, fun"

"Sure, sure sure" slurred Dr Gum with his triple sherbet treat, the three pretty blonde bombshells all in a row.

"Well she's got her daddy's C&C (car) and she's cruisin' through the harbor strait (hamburger stand) now, she forgot all about the library like she told her old man now, And with the radio blastin' she goes cruisin' just as fast as she can now, and she'll have fun fun fun till daddy takes the C& C (T-bird) away….."

Cali reflected on her father's fortunes, he was never there for her, he had taken away a vital part of her child-hood. Stolen it like Robin Hood, robbing from the rich to pay for the poor plantation workers, the pawns in his powerful net-work. In the process he had neglected his own flesh and blood.

"I still can't fathom how I could be so stupid. I let the 'lone ranger' get away!"

"Get over it!" snapped Stacy, as the band stopped." Cali caught wind of her outburst and recognized Arthur. "You're so generous! they even reciprocated and restored your set of wheels!"

stated Stacy. The first set flew by as the band cut for a quick break.

Cali came over to greet the mysterious comical conga man.

"Do you remember me?" she asked

Arthur's heart fluttered then said flirtatiously,

"You look smashing, I mean your music is smashing!"

"Thanks, I didn't get your name last time, at the club in Tijuana...Do you remember?"

"I'll leave you two to get reacquainted, I have to go powder my nose" whispered Stacy in Arthur's ear, then dashed off ere he could introduce her. She didn't feel threatened by the sexy singin' senorita, but she'd hurry back

"Hasta la vista!"

Arthur diverted his attention to the alluring beach babe.

"As I recall, I riled a rather boorish muscled bound beach bum. Before I knew it, my head was bouncing around the inside of a bongo drum....I had a case of sanilocity."

"Sanilocity? Like Travelocity?"

"Lapse or loss of sanity" slurred Arthur

incoherently.

"So what brings you to Cabos?" she asked thoroughly confused by this buffoon. Not a clue as to his career.

"I see you got a souvenir?" she asked." May I ?" as she offered to sign in a curious chicken scratch.

"It's Cali-graphy."

"Ha, ha" she laughed.

"So are you and the misses here on a honey-moon?"

"Oh, you mean? No she's my private nurse, appointed after the accident."

"Oh" stated Cali excitedly.

"So you're not?"

"No, just out for some R and R."

"Rest and relaxation?"

"No Reelin' and Reelin'."

Cali was confused but even more curious about the catch phrase.

"Reel, as in the Bisbee's tourney and 'reel' as in films, motion pictures."

"Motion pictures? You're one of those big shot Beverly Hills film producers, aren't you?"

"Well you're getting warmer. I'm here to

remake an old classic, I have a few concepts I've been toying with..."

"I'll be staying at the 'Hotel California, why don't we meet later?"

"That's a long trip. I suppose you have your private jet parked on the landing pad at San Jose airport to whisk you back and forth?"

She didn't know where he was coming from.

"No, dummy, the 'Hotel Cali-fornia', it's just up the road in Todos Santos."

"You don't say, I thought you meant The Hotel California. All you rock stars must know the cover to the Eagle's album, is the real 'Beverly Hills' hotel." Arthur's wheels were beginning to spin again.

"You know, you've just given me a great idea, in fact you may be the answer to my prayer." He tried to reach out and and puckered up.

"Cali" called one of the Crooners from the stage. She dashed off before he could peck her on the cheek.

"Hooty?" asked Stacy comically as she arrived at the table.

"Howdy."

"You look like a blowfish" she laughed.

The band revved up with another round, breakin' the waitin' audience,

"If everybody had an ocean Across the U. S. A. then everybody'd be surfin' Like Californi-a You'd see 'em wearing their baggies Huarachi sandals too A bushy bushy blonde hairdo…" Several bunnies shook their heads striking Dr Gum with their long manes. "Fishin' Cabo Way. You'd catch em fishin' at Del Mar, Ventura county line, Santa Cruz and Trestle, Australia's Narrabeen, All over Manhattan and down Doheny way, Everybody's gone fishin' fishin' Cabo Way." The crowd went wild in their contorted theatrics, torn between surf moves and spinning their arms in front of them as if reeling in their dance partner. They were having some 'reel' fun. The Crooners left Cali with another spankin' solo, her aggressiveness nurtured from her emulation of Madonna she defiantly belted out several bars of 'Papa Don't Preach', "The one you said I could do without, We're in an awful mess, And I don't mean maybe please papa don't preach , I'm in trouble deep papa don't preach I've been losing sleep …..oh don't you stop loving me daddy…."

Arthur drifted from Stacy's idle chatter and eyed his starlet. He knew he had found a winner.

"How does HCFC sound?"

"Sounds like a loan shark, or lending institute, or bank" said Stacy astutely.

"Ho-tel Cali-fornia Film Com-pany'" articulated Arthur awfully slowly.

"You don't say?" mimicked his mistress at an even slower pace.

"When did you come up with this? It's brilli-ant."

"I don't know, the words kept calling me back" as he peered right through Stacy at his inspiration."

"Do you know what you're getting yourself into?"

"Definitely! A dynamic duo."

Stacy sensed her death knell, Arthur 'd likely toss her like baggage, flotsam and jetsom. Their steamy affair just a bewildering Baja fling. The Cadillac Crooners finished the set with 'Help me, Rhonda' "Well since She put me down I've been out doin' in my head, Come in late at night and in the morning I just lay in bed, Well Rhonda you just look so fine, look so fine, And I know it wouldn't take much time, For you to help me Rhonda, Help me get her out of my heart, Help me Rhonda, help help me Rhonda, Help me Rhonda, help help me Rhonda .....Help me Rhonda yeah, Get her out of my heart...."

Cali understood, the golden opportunity may not come up again. She stormed over to Arthur as the Crooners set down their instruments and confronted Stacy.

"Stacy, I'd like you to meet Cali."

"Cali, Arthur hasn't mentioned you before."

"I'm the new kid in town" she said toying with Stacy.

"I hope this town is big enough for the both of you" said Arthur sensing a cat fight. Dr Gum sauntered by their table like a mesmerized magician with not one but three bunnies in his arms.

"Hat's off to you Dr Gum" greeted Arthur.

"Ah, I see the casting director is here" ribbed Dr Gum noticing the auto-graphed cast. "Perhaps you'd care to strap your rod onto it, you'd have the biggest casting rod in Cabos."

The girls chuckled briefly.

"Casting director? We'd love to be in your film" cooed the bubbly co-ed playboy playmates.

"Well, the cat's out of the bag, word sure travels fast in these parts, Must be the Santa Ana winds, the motion picture idea is certainly gaining momentum."

"Do you have a script?" asked a bodacious bombshell just happening to pass by.

"Consuela? I'm so glad you could come" conferred Cali.

"The more the merrier" said Arthur. "I was tossing a few scripts around."

"The one armed bandit? Er juggler? Now I've seen everything" joked Dr Gum. Cali offered her two cents worth.

"I have an idea" offered Cali. The group gathered around. "'La Perla'"

"The pearl? " asked Arthur intrigued by the title.

"It's a classic Mexican tale. The Pearl, by one of the best known American writers, John Steinbeck."

"Hmmmm" mulled Arthur, go on."

"It is the story of a little boy, Coyo -tito, who is

stung by a scorpion. Their family is too poor to pay for a doctor. Juano and Kino take their family pearl diving. Juano's prayers are answered when Kino surfaces with the biggest pearl he has ever seen, the 'Pearl of the World'."

"The mother of all pearls" slurred Arthur.

"Shhh!" silenced Stacy.

"Kino is making a 'wish list' of all the things they can now afford. The doctor hears of his discovery and comes to cure Coyotito. Kino however hides the pearl under the floor boards, intent on selling it to the local pearl merchants. Juano realizes the pearl is bringing evil and decides to throw it back. Kino slaps her. A mysterious man attacks them. Kino kills the man in self defense. They escape and hide in a cave. They return to find their house burned to the ground. Coyotito howls like a coyote in a sneak attack but is killed. Juano carries her dead son in her shawl. Kino is so enraged he kills all of them. In the end he tosses the pearl back, he has given up hope!"

"It's a rather sinister screenplay" surmised Stacy.

"Don't you see? It's a statement about how new

wealth can corrupt the soul, the longing for money will corrupt all that is good."

"I like it, money is not the root of all evil, but the love of it is. It mustn't be idolized" said Dr Gum. "It can bring great joy or tremendous tragedy."

"Oh cry me a river" said Arthur. "We're here at the Wabo, to welcome in the week's festivities. A toast to wealth!"

"Here, here, but first and foremost health and happiness!" stated Dr Gum.

"Al right St Luke Skywalker" snarled Arthur. Let's see who brings in biggest snatch, uh catch" as he ogled the girls slobbering all over the table.

"Garcon bring me another 'hooker'." The Waban waiter brought a 150 proof pure rum.

"Gracios" Arthur poured everyone a shot glass spilling between the rims.

"May the best man win, Arthur."

Cali had left to resume and round out the evening with her last set. Some of the Wabans were wobbling as they wandered out of the club. Most stayed into the wee hours of the morning. The tune 'Summer in Paradise' struck a few sensitive chords, yet Cali felt she might get through to the movie moguls. "Paradise is a state of mind where Mother Nature nurtures and man is kind, We need a change now wouldn't it be nice if we could bring back summer….too much consumption too much greed, when you consider all the people livin' in need interdependence in this world is a natural fact And we're all under attack…it's the eve of destruction or so they say, But mankind doesn't have to go that way, If we all get together we can make things right, And we can bring back summer, Get back our summer, Summer in Paradise, Summer in Paradise…"

The remainder of the set was but a blur for most. The music's beats , the countless marguerita's had soothed the savage beasts, the sailors and their sexy first mates. Cali came back to bid the tycoons adieu, about to embark on their seafaring sail fishing adventure in the morn'.

"At least give it a thought. Sleep on it" he suggested.

"When can I see you again?" asked Arthur as he stumbled and nearly knocked Stacy over. He was smitten.

"You'll know where to find me."

"The Hotel California?" he questioned. "But that's hours from here, I can't go back to California without making a picture." Arthur wasn't making any sense. He had been drinkin' doubles and talking stupid the remainder of the evening.

"I'll meet you at the marina" said Cali. "To-morrow afternoon."

"You had better brace him before he falls into the briny drink" warned Cali.

"I'll stay on top of things" agreed Stacy.

Dr Gum teetered while his bunnies tottered, somehow they stayed on their feet in a curiously choreographed Cabo Wobble along the water's edge.

19: Playing Hooky

"A vacation is what you take
when you can no longer take
what you've been taking."
- Earl Wilson

As the Spanish armada may have set sail for the new land, the fishing fleet, ranging from the cushy 180' cabin cruisers to small antiquated aluminum out boards, rounded land's end. Most of the bleary eyed fishermen had left the congested 'Marlin Alley' of Cabos before the crack of dawn. Rushing toward their prime targets, the methodically mapped out points on the Mercator grid. Previous years of either a plentiful catch or a prize winning pull had taught them precisely were to cast. Cali in her customary morning ritual cruised along the picturesque marina. More than 1200 boats surged through the narrow opening into the harbor each year. In days of yore, a few English pirates sought shelter there planning their plunders on Manila merchant ships. In the 1930's a small fishing village thrived on 'cannery row'. The fishing craze of the 50's and 60's put Cabos on the map. Wealthy rabid anglers were lured from around the world. Today, larger cruise liners anchor in the deep waters of Bahia de Cabos San Lucas, then shuttle their passengers to the busy downtown port. Cali eyed a large cruiser, moored in the desolate tranquil marina, save for the curious cackle of a few sea gulls frolicking on the hitching posts.

"Odd" mused Cali, "almost everyone else has gone for the day, perhaps they had engine troubles or simply over slept and decided to extend the siesta for the whole day." She decided to take a stroll along the landing to get a closer look. It was such a beautiful morning, "maybe I can catch a lift later this afternoon?"

The Boa, firmly tied to the dock, sat rigidly cushioned against a few old retreaded tires. One of the deck hands was scrubbing a filthy bloody muddy mess from the stern and after compartment. Cali wondered if these anglers were in actuality the early risers, the early birds who had already caught the biggest worm? Sure that's it! They are cleaning their catch, scrubbing the poop deck, preparing for the next act and outing, removing the bloody entrails from the loser lured into a fierce yet fool hardy futile struggle, just like the belligerent bull blinded by the bandeleros bold moves motioning them into position for the macabre thrust of their blades.

"Hey, gringo, you missed a spot, I'm not paying you to play around in the bahia." snapped the cranky captain or coworker. The sweating sailor dunked the dripping red mop into the bucket, then heaved it over the stern of the boat. Cali was caught by a spray of errant extra sudsy liquid. She rubbed her eyes and wiped her cheek in shock, then spit out the bloody salty swill.

"Sorry miss, I didn't see you standing there" said the scrubber.

"It's alright" Cali blinked a couple of times, then stood with a blank expression for several minutes.

"Hey, senorita, you sure you're al-right, you look like you've seen a ghost-ship!" D-R-E-A-M-W-E-A-V-E-R, the letters leapt through her agonizing milieu of memories, carefully archived. Cali touched her cheek, it sent a shock wave through her entire body.

"You catching cold miss? the cool Pacific morning mist will do that to you, if you're not acclimatized."

Acclimatized? Nothing in the world could have prepared her for this coincidence. The last word she remembered after she was nearly dragged to her death so many years ago. Her fateful swim – ming trip, the anglers off Avalon. It came back to her in a flash. The creator must have a sick twisted sense of humor bringing her here. Was she simply a puppet or pawn, to play out part of the master plan? 'I've come not to bring peace, but to bring a sword' (Matthew 10: 34-39 and Luke 12: 49-53 parallels) The very words spoken by Jesus himself advocating vengeance and violence in a just war?

Literally, she was to take a sword, as the valiant knights of the round table had on their crusades. Cali burned in a surreal sort of way like a hypnotic drug induced rage or demon possessed drug worshipper. I mustn't "Snap!" she convinced herself as she uttered the latter word out loud.

"Snapper? Yeah we caught plenty of those, most we had to unhook and release, they didn't meet the minimum requirement of 300 lbs."

Mimimum requirement? Just like she had been flung off the deck, a scrawny child squirming for her life. Not a thought or care about throwing her a lifeline! Simply discarded as human trash, effluent of the very affluent drug lords, raping the people and the land with their illicit crops in their perpetual pursuit of pleasure. Cali, she thought to herself, you have to play your cards right. After all, you may be over reacting. You have to have proof it's the same boat, the same men that did this to you. Perhaps, all the excitement, a small taste of success with the crooners had gone to her head. That's it, it's the tequila talking again!

The gritty gringo burnished the gold and black stenciled letters and spit one last time for good measure as he wipe the stern to a smooth shimmering shine.

"Ain't she a beauty?" asked the deck hand proud of his elbow grease effort.

"She sure is" yelled his partner in crime perched atop the control panel. "Ask her aboard."

"Oh, si," he said oblivious of his double entendre. "You like to go for a ride miss?"

Cali tread carefully in the shark infested waters. The crew more crafty and cruel than the worst deep sea carnivore. At least it would have finished the job and chewed her to pieces in a quick painless death and not spit her out and discard-
ed her so callously.

"Are you boys going out again? Why aren't you out with the other anglers, playing a little hooky are we?"

"We could ask you the same thing, you're certainly too pretty to be abandoned by your crew. Such fools."

Look who's talking she mused.

"We just arrived from Acapulco, we'll slowly mosey along the coast of Mexico, work our way to San Diego and Los Angeles."

“That’s a long trip, isn’t it?”

“Nah, just a hop, skip and a jump, one leg of a much longer voyage.”

“Voyage?”

“Si, from Buenaventura to Puerto Amuelleras, Panama then up the coast.”

“What’s all the racquet?” came a crusty call from below deck.

“Go back to sleep” said the captain, or the most confident desperado topside.

“I thought I heard another woman with a distinct American accent. What’s she doing here?” stated the cheeky Chiquita.

“Please, Penelope, be a little more hospitable to our guest…..”

“Cali, Cali Columbia.”

“No, are you pulling my leg?” asked Penelope.

“No, that’s my real given name. My father was from there, my mother, well, she was an American actress.”

“Your father?”

“Yes, Victor Hidalgo Columbia, you have heard of him?”

“Not, the Victor Columbia?”

"I wasn't aware that he had gained such notoriety?"

"You're not talking about the exiled cartel leader? He may have even been our employer at one time."

"Exiled?"

"Figure of speech, his whereabouts are unknown, some say he went inland, some say he left the country. The heat was on as the Columbian police clamped down on the big fish. Most were caught."

"So now you've joined the cause so to speak? Are you catching the big ones?"

"Ha, ha, she is funny Pedro, non?" A few more disheveled damsels crept from the downstairs boudoir. They looked like all the others Cali had confronted at the Hotel California. Beautiful, bewildered women, resorting to turning a few tricks. Tossed by their bosses, to eke out a living in the small haciendas or hovels all along the coast.

"How are things in Buenaventura by the way?" she probed. Any life would be better than existing there. Caught in the cross fire in an armed coupe by the guerillas or highly sophisticated offensives by the Archangel Henao for control of the island. She too would prefer a mass exodus from the killing fields if given the choice.

"Bad, but we get by!"

"Getting by? Looks like you have quite the little flagship here."

"Yes, a modest aging member of the fleet."

"Fleet?"

"Our little armada constantly caters to the very rich. The fortunate few who can follow their dreams elsewhere."

"You're the dream weaver?"

"Pepe, Pepe Gonzalez, at your service senorita" said the crusty sea dog in a scratchy voice as he removed his hat and waved it in front of his unshaven features. His cigar stuck between his lips like a permanent fixture.

"Penelope why don't you pour us a few drinks?"

"This early, it's only after eight."

"Santa Maria, where's your sense of hospitality? Do unto others" he said facetiously. Cali was stunned by the remark She was not yet convinced these were the same soulless men who had dumped her.

"Si"

"Pedro, help her aboard."

"Si senor" The seamen reached out his bloody paw, quickly wiping it in the process. His muscular frame, much like the amorous bullfighter she had met, flung her aboard. A stable of fine fillets crept onto the deck in various states of undress,
one more beautiful and buxom than the next."

"Quite the collection you have caught Pepe, a couple of P's in a pod."

"Ha, she is so funny" laughed his scrubber slightly hunched over. The ogre ogled the other women, insuring they didn't jump ship just yet.

"We're not Charlie's angels if that's what you're thinking" stated Penelope proud of her physique and prowess. Pleasure is our game, we keep everyone who can afford to pay happy."

"I bet you can" said Cali callously.

"A girl has to do what a girl has to do."

Cali concurred retracing her own convoluted steps to this intriguing intersection in her life.

"But it's only temporary!"

"Something to pass the time?"

"You could say that. We're all just passing

through to, how do you say? greener pastures."

"Just good grazin' here?"

"We all have to eat!"

"Girls please" said Pepe preventing a predicament.

"So you must have plenty of fresh fish, by the look of it?" questioned Cali.

"We just got rid of our 'bait' of sardines. We were informed that mackerel work best here in Cabos."

"Oh you've been scouring the favorite fishing spots?"

"Oh just La Paz and Loreto."

"They say in Tapijulapa, Tabasco the 'Pesca de la Sardines', a cave, the cave of the sardines, the more sardines you catch, the more rain falls on the crops."

"On everyone a little rain must fall, senorita" he said sinisterly. Cali felt uncomfortable, like she'd smelled a rat.

"Here you are miss." Penelope offered a beautiful floral bouquet, the tray brimming with fresh fruit, lemons, limes. A few upended tequila shot glasses were stacked in the middle like a glass light house. The shiny glasses reflected the sunlight creeping over the rocky crags on the west side of town jutting into the bay towards land's end.

"So you think the grass is greener on this side of the equator?" asked Cali coldly.

"The girls have big plans" insisted Pepe, they're going to be movie stars" he chuckled callously.

"Si" they said excitedly, slugging back the strong drink.

"Just like you promised."

"Promised?"

"Some of the girls have their sights set on Hollywood" he said facetiously.

"They are beautiful. Are those natural?" asked Cali as she placed her empty shooter glass on the tray.

"Go ahead" said Penelope. Cali fished around the tray and found a swizzle stick. She gently poked the plentiful package protruding from the tiny tightly strung bikini top.

"Use your hands, here" she grabbed her wrist and placed Cali's palm on the merchandise."

"They feel so firm, full, wonder-fully soft.

They're perfect."

"Thanks to Dr Pitanguy, or some of his disciples down in Buenaventura."

"But I thought you....."

"The last of the clinics closed as we left. Even the surgeons felt uncomfortable, their lives constantly threatened. One doctor nearly had his throat slit just before he closed shop. It just wasn't worth the risk."

"Too bad. But you are all so very beautiful."

"Gracios, you can thank Pepe, he paid for them."

"No."

"Si, Pepe takes care of his mistresses. "They always make it up to me in time."

"Quite the father figure Pepe, a real Sugar Daddy?" congratulated Cali.

"Perhaps you would like Pepe to take care of you?"

"In time" toyed Cali.

"But such talent and beauty should not go to waste" began Cali. The girls and crew were intrigued.

"What do you mean?"

"You ought to be playmates, or perhaps in .....pictures"

"Now you're talking" said pedro.

"And you know a way?"

"Pepe, where there's a will, there's always a way!" said Cali intent on meting revenge as soon as she could prove her theory. "I know of a big movie mogul who is making a motion picture here in Mexico."

"Non!"

"Si, he has deep pockets but his search for a real star has eluded him. Much like the big one that all the fishermen are floundering around out there for."

"I am planning to meet him here on the marina, when he returns this afternoon."

"Perhaps Pepe can play a small role?"

"You have to think bigger Pepe, don't you want a piece of the action, a really big piece of the pie, say co-producer?"

"Where did this angel come from?" asked the perplexed fisherman.

"Thank Pedro, he reeled me in."

“Ha, ha, ha” laughed the other women, stars glimmering in their glassy glazed eyes.

“I have suggested a film to him, you might be interested in the story line…”

“Let’s hear it” pleaded Penelope. Cali told the callous tale of ‘The Pearl’, and how the prize had been returned to the sea. The others laughed at the idea.

“Right now, everything she’s said sounds like a bloody fish story.”

“We’ll see who has the last laugh in time” suggested Cali.

20: A Fine Catch

"The best kind of prize is a 'sur'prise. It has to be really big, cause you know you can film an ordinary sized man and he comes out looking this big."
- Willy Wonka.

The entire crew latched onto either side of Arthur's customized barber chair trying to weight him down. They feared that the brass mountings would shear, he and his throne would be yanked into the briny deep.

"Ease some slack Arthur" pleaded the seasoned Mexican fishermen. They perspired profusely fighting for Arthur's life and their reputations.

Arthur's cast began to crack, the rod firmly fastened by neoprene straps. The ingeniously attached reel allowed Arthur to enjoy himself while simply resting his elbows on the wide leather hand-rail. The sturdy barber chair, circa 1800 swiveled freely as a gimbel as the boat kept a steady heading. By applying pressure, he could raise himself above the rest of the crew. A position he was accustomed to. However, he had reached the limit of the chair, even the steel pole was about to snap.

"What the hell have I caught, Moby Dick?" questioned Arthur. "Get me out of here."

"You've probably hit the magic mark."

"At least a thousand pounder."

"For the love of.."

"Relax, just let out a little more line, we've got all day. We'll simply tire him out!" they laughed nervously about to go into the drink.

"I'll lose my arm, for God's sake" shouted Arthur as several fracture lines appeared around the massive trunk.

"Well have to remove the rod from his cast before the marlin breaks it off." yelled the Mexican captain.

"You'll never forget this Arthur, I swear."

"If I live to tell about it. No one will believe me anyway. Talk about bad beginner's luck." I'll be surfing behind Moby Dick before you can say Captain Ahab"

"On the count of three you release the rod"

"Right."

"One, two..." The cast cracked like a twig as the mighty anglers grabbed the rod. The incredible strength of the line refused to give. They'd have to out wrestle the wily sailfish, which showed no sign of giving up. The men eased it from Arthur's arm, in all the commotion, the one arm bandit was spun wildly. If it weren't for the tenuous grip of the weathered mounts, Arthur would have sailed into orbit like a corkscrew or wind up spin top. His leg caught one unwary fisherman in the groin which sent him flying prostrate to the deck. The other two hung on for dear life. Vertigo overcame Arthur, he passed out from the excessive G forces.

"Santa Maria!" shouted the amazed men, the two amazed amigos were surprised they were still hanging on. The third gringo groaned in pain floundering around on the poop deck, like a victim of Montezuma's revenge. The other two agile anglers braced themselves against the stern of the boat. The appeared like two America's Cup team mates leaning off the deck in a brisk breeze, only in reverse, in board!

"I'll keep my motor running!" shouted the captain from the control console or we'll be pulled under!"

"Si!" shouted the squirming sweating sailors. If they relinquished their grip now, they'd lose rod reel and the purse. They figured they had a fortune slowly yanking the rod from their fatigued fingertips. Probably the grand prize of a few million, a once in a lifetime catch.

"We're not going to give up Arthur."

"That's' the spirit" he shouted as he climbed the rail with his free hand up to the stash of tequila on the upper deck.

"Carry on Catching!" quipped Arthur comically.

"Like I always said 'there's quality and then there's quality'."

"Si senor, we won't need to go out again if we can find a way to reel him in."

"I meant the tequila, we can't run a dry ship."

"I don't think you realize the extent of our escapade."

"Oh and what is that?"

"You've landed yourself a thousand pounder, and you say this is your very first attempt?"

"Couldn't be bothered, I can have the finest caviar flown in at the drop of a hat." The captain fumed.

"Do you realize some of us will scour the ocean our entire lives and never eye anything remotely this big."

"Aye, aye capitane. Perhaps you should take up trawling" he said with a southern drawl."

"But where's the fun in that? The thrill of the chase?"

"'Chase schmace, if you can't beat 'em, join 'em, 20,000 leagues under the sea, just scoop them up, scoo be doo" Arthur began to slur and stutter his words. He was well on his way to another alcohol -lic afternoon of delirious delights.

"You'll make our team very proud, you just wait and see."

"See? Remind me to use dynamite depth charges next time. Only the sonar knows where they are actually hiding!"

"That's against the rules of the competition" queried the captain "As is angular angling."

"Angle your…"

"Stealing someone else's fish right from under their noses. Some previous 'professionals' prefer to simply snip the line and claim the hooked fish. Why I wouldn't be surprised to find small sub-mersibles snagging the really big sailfish."

"Captain Nemo himself, I presume to claim first prize?"

"Precisely."

"Well if this has all been a waste of time, I'll drink to that, In fact, let's all get drunk and get wasted, I'm having the time of my life!" said Arthur reasonably well. "I must be sobering up, I actually made sense. Another round gringo! We shan't let a drop of tequila go to waste." The captain passed the bottle to Arthur's free arm. The crew encountered another sudden tug on the taut line. The bottle disappeared over the side.

"Don't worry, willy or marly the marlin, or sally the sailfish needs it more than I do. I think their time's nearly up!"

"You might be right"

"Captain" shouted the two amigos, we need some help, pronto!"

"Here, hang onto the wheel, just don't touch anything Arthur."

"Aye aye, Captain, wait a minute, I'm the Captain now." he grabbed the cap as the pilot stepped down the vertical incline. "Captain Arthur, it has a flashy ring to it" surmised the soused sea dog. Arthur leaned back and struck the throttle, the captain flew off the back of the boat as he approached the two exhausted anglers appearing to fight for possession of the rod.

"Man overboard!" they shouted. Arthur was oblivious to their antics. They kept pointing to the stern.

"Yes, I can see you've caught it. fishy, fishy, here fishy fishy!" His cast caught the left throttle as he turned back

"I'm caught" said Arthur trying to free himself. He continue to tug the cast, the large crack in the cast had wrapped itself onto the left knob. He pulled frantically to free his arm. The lever retracted and sent the vessel into a hard to port turn

In fact they were coming about, full circle.
The bewildered crew thanked Arthur for caring for their compadre.

"Gracios, gringo, gracios!" The tiny cap bobbing in the water came into range. An arm shot up and shook wildly to attempt to attract attention.

"What the…?" shouted the captain as he swallowed a mouthful of warm salty water. 'Lady Luck' was on his starboard side and steadily constricted her circle. She had him clearly in his sights.

"Wee" shouted Arthur unaware of the accident about to occur abaft.

The circular motion took it's toll on everyone, it must've confused the massive marlin the most, for the Mexicans felt the tension subside. Only 8 hours of sheer 'enjoyment'.

"Santo Christopher, it's a miracle" shouted the fishermen falling to their knees. The captain climbed aboard the aft sea level deck. One more incident and he'd step off for good he swore in a form of Spanish.

He helped reel in the former foe, the giant fish exhausted from the tail spin, had suddenly expired.

Miles of the 15 X stronger than steel line looked frayed.

"Did you get him?" asked Arthur.

"Yes we got him" The captain shook his fist at Arthur soaking, slip sliding away.

"How big is he?"

"Oh about six feet of steamin' mad Mexican…."

"I thought we had at least a ten footer" They were all finally on the same page, as the giant foil of the sword fish popped out of the water like a periscope. The heavy hook had caught the gills and ground it's way back toward the tip of his sword.

"He didn't stand a chance!"

"Poor fishy!" Arthur extended his apologies. It took all hands on deck to hook the fish.

"Arthur can you give us a hand?" they pleaded.

"I suppose you'd like me to meet someone?"

"All 16'– 20'of him, in fact."

"My God, it's a giant can opener" he said.

"Grab a hold and steady the beast, we'll reel him in. Mama mia, it's the mother of all marlin!" surmised the surprised sailor.

"How do you know it's a female?" asked Arthur casually.

“Have you ever seen anything that big?”

“Never in my wildest dreams…”

“I don’t know what all the fuss is about. You’ll need a chainsaw to filet this tuna.”

“We could feed the entire Spanish Armada with the meat on this whopper!”

“It’s a bloody whale for God’s sake, You’d better see if anyone’s living in there” asked Arthur facetiously. “He must have had his own postal code!”

“Is there ever a time when a serious word slips through those lips of yours Arthur?”

“Only when I’m drunk.”

“I’ll hand it to you Arthur it was well worth the wait, wasn’t it?”

“I’ll say!” Arthur slipped the soggy remnants of the cast from his arm. “No, I’ve got to hand it to you” The crew roared in hysterical conniptions as he gave the dripping captain his soaked mushy cast.

“We have to get that in a sling ASAP” suggested the captain.

“Would that be a Singapore sling?”

“Shut up Arthur!” snapped the captain “Or I’ll

wrap this neoprene wrap around your neck!"

"Aye , aye" The conniving captain quickly removed the end of the rod. He wrapped a small pillow around Arthur's wrist then wound the neoprene bungy like chord around his arm. "It'll have to suffice! Sorry no hook, Captain!"

"It's bound to sting, when the tequila wears off. You might want to see a doctor in town when we get back. Get it cast."

"By all means, I'm still the casting director, aren't I?" The crew nearly broke out in tears as they rolled around gripping their guts.

"You ought to be in the movies! This is one Ripley's believe it or not tale that should have been recorded on film!"

"How right you are."

"I don't think there is a stuntman alive who could replicate this reelin' rodeo ride."

"You certainly have a point."

"Not as much as our foiled bustin' bronco barracuda here."

"It's a swordfish."

"Was."

"Potato, Pinata, Patatoe" Arthur was in his prime

time comedy mode.

“Aren’t you glad you skipped out on your boring lecture?”

“Wouldn’t have missed this for the world. A pound of tuna is worth a ton of theory I always say!” speculated Arthur.

“Have you ever thought of doing stand up comedy?” asked the curios crew.

“I did but I could never stand up long enough to tell a joke. My entire life is a joke.” sulked Arthur. ”I might as well have a silver spoon installed where the Captain would affix his hook. I’m a failure! My billionaire father Sperry Sr. has made a fortune in films. He’ll cut me off if I so much as think of crossing the Rio Grande line and produce anything in Mexico.”

“What a miserable…..”

“Why, not only do you have the biggest fish to grace these waters, the best fish story as long as I can remember, but you ‘ll soon have the purse, a cool 3-4 million for Sammy the swordfish.”

“You don’t say?”

“It will certainly kick start a full length feature in this neck of the desert.”

"Why, we can call up all our aunts and uncles, brothers, sisters….. you'll have the entire cast, all in the family."

"Fantastic! Fantastic! You're brilliant amigo!"

"And you'll have done it all on your own."

"By my own hook!" he laughed as he ogled his padded prosthesis protruding from his elbow.

"By your own hook."

"This calls for a toast" The amigos agreed as they continued to drift in the oscillating ocean waves.

"Here's to playing hooky!"

"To beginner's luck."

"To our future fortunes in the Mexican film industry."

"And to many more pieces of tail"

"Aye, Aye Arthur!"

"Now let's set a course for Cabos full speed ahead and collect our prize money before the ship is plundered by pirates.

21: By Hook or Crook

> "Who cares if they say we've gone 'round the bend, it's our lives that we lead it's on us that we depend, And the visions that we see, let us see them again and again."
>
> - Lee Murdock, 'The Captain and the Mystic'

The other conference attendees certainly noticed Arthur's absence.

"That Arthur!" fumed the hostess.

Another typical no show. As he had so comically stated in his senior years, 'if I wouldn't have attended this lecture I would have received 100%!'

As the last of the fishing fleet returned, even the

Cabos Coast Guard was beginning to fret. "Still no sign of the 'Lucky Lady' sir!" remarked Garcia as the harbor lights began to twinkle. "Wait, I think I see her now. Yes, there she is coming around the pinnacle at land's end."

"I was about to call in the big guns." A crowd had gathered on the dock expecting to catch a glimpse of the 'big one'. Rumor had it that a novice angler on his first outing had reeled in the mother of all marlin. The LL slowly squeezed into her berth as she rounded the bend in the bay. The forlorn fatigued fishermen had enough strength to muster a mighty big grin.

"It's huge!" commented the curious chiquitas, leaning over the rail of the 'Dreamweaver' docked in the neighboring stall.

"What happened to your cast? I thought you were the casting director?" inquired the clueless bunnies bouncing down the landing.

"Arthur?" shouted Cali, "it wasn't you, was it? Just between us…"

"It was a fierce battle" Arthur began his tyrade. "The tiny ship was tossed, if not for the courage of the fearless crew the marlin may …." He looked at the stunned anglers. "I'm the king of the Cabos castle you're all the empty handed vassels" spewed out Arthur in a venomous intoxicated state.

"That's quite enough Arthur. Let's quit while we're ahead!" suggested the humble Mexican captain. "I'll be back for more. Only this time I'll catch a fish, You can give this one to the peasants, let them eat fish."

"He's just kidding folks, Help me Pedro, we'll weigh him in. Perhaps one of you pretties can quietly escort Arthur off the premises?"

"Sure!" before he was inundated by hysterical high strung senoritas, Cali grabbed his unimpeded arm and pulled him onto the 'Dreamweaver'. The other women heaved him onto the deck like a rock star flung into a crowd of fans.

"Lucky for you, we happened to be in the neighborhood" said Pepe intent on meeting the mogul. Some big shot? he mused. This anonymous busker certainly had the others fooled. A real shark. He liked strong drink like himself, lucky with the ladies. Pepe knew he had met his partner in crime.

"Well, what did I tell you?" Cali asked the shady businessmen, weaving a carefully crafted scenario of her own.

"Arthur I'd like you to meet Pepe."

"Please to meet you Pay Pay" exaggerating the accent. "What is your saying?.. 'Birds of a feather.... Flock together'".

"Well I must say, your craft is adorned in the most exquisite plumage" complimented Arthur admiring the adoring onlookers.

"Why thank you, senor."

"Call me Arthur, Sir Arthur."

"Si sir."

"But back to business, as I was saying, I understand you are scouting for a location to shoot your next full length feature film?"

Cali had embellished his intentions for dramatic effect and bank roll ability.

"Yes, she's truly been an inspiration" his wheels were always turning. "in fact she had given me the concept. It just came to me." The other women wanted in on the action. Penelope approached Arthur and perched herself on his lap.

"Tell me more my charming prince" she pleaded

with the aspiring producer.

"Well if you insist" she licked his earlobe. "I think I feel a nibble again. Maybe I'll reel in another big one?"

"Careful what you wish for, you're dreams may come true" said Penelope slyly. Cali shrugged off her advances. She feared it was simply part of the cleverly crafted theatrics, to snare and entrap Arthur, oblivious to the cartels cruel true intentions. He may simply be another pawn in the power struggle. She was all too familiar with their shady business practices. Arthur was merely a fish caught in their slippery crime network out of the frying pan soon into the line of cross fire. They had to watch their step.

"What are you going to do with your share of the prize money?" asked Pepe.

"The crew suggested I bankroll a film with local talent."

"Excellent idea" lauded Pepe. "Look around you, I can provide you with all the props you need."

"Props? Is that all we are to you?" fume Penelope. We're professionals."

"There's only one catch, a hook."

"Si?"

"My father mustn't know that I'm shooting in Mexico. He'll only bankroll a film of his own in America."

"And that is a problemo?"

"This is where Cali comes into the picture. We've formed the HCFC, the 'Hotel California Film Company'. I found some hotel stationary from the Beverly Hills Hotel. My staff was talent scouting."

"Yes, go on" insisted Pepe perkier than usual."

"We have enough film footage to create the illusion that the film is taking place there or at the Del, the grand dame in San Diego. In fact it is where I first set eyes on this lovely creature. I'm not quite convinced that 'La Perla' is the right picture to produce?"

"In my opinion, you take your time. You take all the action shots you like senor, then the highly gifted team of editors trim it and weave a masterpiece. I'll give you all the funding you need. You know a million dollars does not go very far these days."

"Yes, I suppose you're right, my part of the prize money is merely a drop in the bucket?"

"You need a real infusion, injection of cash!" suggested Pepe. "And you know where to find it? Why, do you have some buried treasure, gold dubloon stashed away somewhere?"

"I like dis gringo" stated Pepe.

"No, but I have an endless supply of venture capital. I have a how do you say 'an eternal fountain like the fountain of youth' much like my mistresses."

"Yes they're quite charming."

"What do you say partner?"

"Well I…." Cali knew the slippery snake would lead them further and further into shark infested waters. The grim flash-back of her deadly dive crept back into her mind, over and over again. They had to tread carefully.

"What did I tell you?" gulped Cali concealing her angst. "Isn't he the greatest?" she said facetiously stroking her chin in a curious puzzling way. The memories of her plunge too painful to reproduce.

"It's a deal!" A slippery handshake between the

two tycoons grafted a gruesome foreboding feature as far as Cali was concerned. Arthur's billions combined with the cartel's conniving connections….Cali recalled a sinister saying 'a fool and his money are soon parted'. Who would fool whom in this game of who's who? wondered the worldly owl.

Arthur amused by the wheeling and dealing, simply proposed another toast.

"Here's to the beautiful sea-noritas worthy of a leading role in my feature, and to a successful venture. Fame and fortune for one and all"

"Here, here!" said Pepe lecherously. There were plenty more fish in the sea, as far as he was concerned. He'd eventually reel in the big one. But he felt confident their fortunes would be made on an even keel. Likely land a role himself. His senoritas bound for stardom in the United States. It'd save him a lot of trou-ble, tending to his vast harem in every hacienda and cantina in Baja.

"Why don't we discuss some story lines?" suggested Arthur "at the 'Giggling Marlin' or 'Squid Row'."

"Sure" laughed the bright eyed beauties as the

starlight twinkled in their dazed eyes.

"I have to see a doctor, my arm's killing me! Get a new cast, after all I'm still the casting director" he confirmed.

"Right Pepe, my co-producer?"

"Si senor" Pepe liked his title, it had a distinguished ring to it, unlike his present perilous position. Cali had other premonitions, and decided to join them, drink to forget…"

"Cali! There you are, we've been looking all over for you?" said the elated Crooners. Their pink pearly Cadillac was parked next to the souped up steamin' red mad mag wheeled Mercedes. His Baja pit crew had certainly done a number on the vehicle. His little deuce coupe a sight to behold. Stacy and Dr Gum met the thirsty consortium on their way to the Cabo Wabo.

"Cali, and the Crooners is it?" Dr Gum recognized the band members.

"Let me congratulate you, you sang up quite a storm last night" he shook each of their hands firmly.

"Thanks." Cali felt a strange ting-ling sensation as their life lines merged in the palm of their hands.

"Have we met before?" she asked, his hands seemed to signify a strange somber significance which Cali couldn't quite place.

"I saw you up in Tijuana, you and the boys were terrific!"

"Yeah that must be it" she mulled over mesmerized.

"You have your work cut out for you Dr Gum" ribbed Arthur. "Bet you can't catch me! I mean catch as big a…"

"You're a tough act to follow. You may have won this round but the battle isn't over yet. I still can't believe you brought it in by yourself. I'd like to have been there!"

"Seeing is believing" slurred Arthur

"Right now I'm seeing double" as he eyed Stacy enveloped in Dr Gum's arms.

Arthur's cell phone vibrated in his pants.

"Son, how's the film business treating you?"

"Fine, just smashing! I've signed a tentative contract with an International consortium. They plan to bankroll the entire film!"

"Splendid, Sperry Jr. Spare me the details. I'll look forward to seeing the final product on the silver screen real soon!"

"Right oh!"

"What's all the racquet in the background, it sounds like you're at a studio. Are they giving you a hard time on the set?"

"No just a few colleagues, smile for the camera." The Cabans gathered around. "Say cheese!" Arthur had embedded a photo of the Beverly Hills Hotel into the back drop, the screen saver of his sophisticated GPS hand set. It always put Sperry Sr at ease, to see a familiar landmark, particular as he returned from a fiercely contested challenge at sea.

"Well say hello to the staff and toast a few stiff ones for me!" Like a few of the seedy senoritas he'd met along the way. Arthur was sure they'd buried more stiffs than the local Mexican under-taker.

"How am I going to pull this off Pepe?" pleaded Arthur.

"Leave the driving to us, senor Arthur. My birds of prey will pray about it. We'll figure something out." His deceptive sly demeanor disguised what was really going on inside that scarred cranium.

Cali sensed it too, ‘silent waters run deep’. Pepe never said much, just like her father and all the newer baby cartel boomers. But once a plan was put into action, they always delivered on their word. She’d have to await the outcome of this convoluted scenario. Her money was riding on Pepe. Arthur was a bumbling buffoon. His luck was bound to run out. Yet she had to be there every step of the way ere Arthur might venture for a long walk off the end of a short pier. Cali knew what shenanigans Pepe and his shifty senoritas were capable of. This couldn’t be the deadly circle Arthur normally dealt with. She placed him in much more elegant, albeit garish grandeur. A lifestyle she could become accustomed to. Was she tiring of the “Crooners’ company? just another page in her colorful history? Perhaps she was approaching a point in her life where she could pen a few songs of her own? Cali had reenacted and mimicked Madonna’s melodies meticulously to a tee. The Beach Boys eternal lyrics etched in the minds of the club’s connoisseurs, yet her interests languished once again. It was time to dance to the tune of a different drummer or dream up her own lyrics. Emulate Arthur's antics with an amusing language not unlike his own jumbled jargon. After all she could pay him no greater compliment than to copy his curious comical style. In her heart, she knew it was a winner, certain to bring the house down! Cali was intent to branch out, on a limb, on her own, change her name, 'Roxy and the Rockettes'? I'll give it some thought she mused. I can change my name, my appearance my accent, my garb in a garish disguise but I can't change my past. It would follow and haunt her forever she feared. Forever destined to bump into lingering memories of her father's tainted existence and her mother's, marked by trouble, turmoil and sanilocity…'loss of sanity' "Good, God I'm beginning to sound like Arthur."

"I hope I don't acquire all his alcoholic habits! What am I saying? I'm no angel! My addictions and consumptive habits, a cornucopia of concoctions and pharmacopoeia, are enough to kill a savage beast. Oh how she wished she could fly away from all this…..leave it all behind, turn a new leaf. Her thoughts bor-dered on suicide as she saw her reflection in the smooth mirror surface of the marina.

"Caught you Cali" humored Arthur as he snuck up behind her on the boardwalk. She shrieked stunned back to consciousness.

"What an a…Arthur. You scared me! You nearly pushed us off into the deep end!"

22: Off the Hook

"You don't always get what you want, but if you try sometimes, you might find, you get what you need."
- Rolling Stones

The midday sun beat upon the two tilted Mexican sombreros as they strolled along the Ave de Cabos San Lucas near the north end of downtown. Stacy held his arm gingerly for the first time since his 'ceremonious' decasting.

"I think the tequila is wearing off" he fretted. I could use a stiff one soon."

"I want you sober so the Spanish doctors can understand you. They have gone through hell helping you before."

They kept their hats at a significant slant to avoid the deadly rays and nearly missed the magnificent structure, the St Luke's/ IMSS Hospital.

"Here we are Arthur, at the ER."

The doors swung open to the modern marvel. A stylishly clad cordial nurse wheeled a tablet PC up to the couple immediately as they came in.

"It look's brand spanking new" said Arthur wedged between the two curvaceous caregivers.

"The 1st of it's kind in Latin America, one of the most unique in the modern world" said the shapely Spanish nurse.

"Your English is simply marvelous" stated Arthur.

"I assisted in Birmingham, with the transfer of the latest Intel technology which you see right here."

"Splendid" said Arthur.

"Everything looks digital" said Stacy surprised, "and I thought we were at the cutting edge."

"You can thank Dr Mariano Gonzalez from Jalisco at the Colored Person Hospital."

"Dr Topete has mentioned him."

"Ah, the top in his field."

"Yes, shall we proceed?"

A series of 3D imaging screens lined the corridor.

"Wow, this looks like a lengthy screening room, or editing suite" said Arthur startled.

The nurse nudged him as she placed a 'You Go' tag on his arm.

"I know where most of my staff would like me to go."

"Please Arthur!" pleaded Stacy equally amazed by the degree of personal attention.

"So you are in the movies?" asked the nurse inquisitively.

"Yes, you won't have to operate?' he asked apprehensively, and leave any-thing on the 'cutting room' floor?"

"Ha, ha, Arthur" said Stacy intent on slapping him.

"No, it's not that serious, I'll simply wrap your arm softly like so…. " Her soft delicate digits went to work applying her artisan craftwork. Arthur's arm was draped in no time. Arthur was very satisfied with the swift service. “Please to meet you, I’m the new casting director, and that’s a wrap!”

“Maria, it was a pleasure meeting you.” The strong stench of tequila had her step back. She wondered who this busker buffoon really was.

“Oh, he’s who he says he is. He could turn this place upside down. Have a series, say ‘St Lukes’ syndicated faster than you could snap your fingers or check him out!” said Stacy facetiously.

“Really?”

“Reel-y!”

“Now now, girls, there’s no point arguing over me “ insisted the dynamic director.

“Mind if we have a peek at your facility?”

“No, by all means. She led them on a quick tour of the 72 bed facility. It ran like a finely tuned swiss clock. More PC’s in place, for personalized service, than Mexico’s Microsoft. Instant info transfer.

“It’s a highly efficient replicable model” said Maria proudly.

“Are there any more nurses as stunning as you?”

“Why thank you Arthur, you’re so sweet”

"You're quite the replicable model yourself" Maria blushed a bright red matching the floral bouquets enlivening the rooms.

"Well, if you do decide to shoot on location, look me up, I'd love to star in your picture. Try to avoid the water for awhile, the cast has to set."

"Sure. Thanks again." Stacy led Arthur down the garden like path along the side streets back toward the marina.

"We were out of there lickety split" said Arthur.

"For what it's worth, I'll have time to hop on the 'Dreamweaver' for one last toss!" as he saw the tall conning tower of the large yacht still tied at it's berth.

"Why bother, you've got this tournament all wrapped up?" snapped Stacy.

"A man's got to do what a man's got to do" he said boldly raising his cast defiantly. She pictured a patch over one of Arthur's eyes, a hook from his plaster stump , and a parrot perched on his left shoulder.

"How true captain."

"Here take the afternoon off" as he tossed her he keys to the bright red sports car parked alongside the marina.

"Thanks" She knew she'd have fun, fun, fun 'til Arthur took the red bird (cardinal?) away."

Arthur hobbled over to the dock.

"Ahoy matees."

"Ah, grand gringo, Mr MGM magnifico!"

"Pepe, my producer and all the my pretty petals, such a lovely bouquet"

"Has he been into the hot sauce again?" asked Penelope softly to a senorita standing next to her.

"Take a whiff."

"You're so unpredictable darling" she said eyeing his shiny white wrap.

"The casting director is back in the saddle"

"I can see that, but why don't you take a siesta?"

"No rest for the wicked."

"Can I come along?" asked Cali strolling along in their neck of the woods.

"The more the merrier" said Pepe as he fired up the engines.

"Robin Hood and his band of merry women" mused Arthur. "Perhaps we can practice our lies, a dry run so to spreak?"

"I have never seen you sober!" said Cali saucily.

"I'll change my wicked ways" he insisted.

"Once a scorpion, always a scorpion"

"But sweetheart, ever since we met, I've become a new man." Cali was not about to get stung again. Her intent was simply to star in a role, however small, then move on. Only time will tell if movies are my forte she mused.

"Shall we?" Arthur tossed the rope ashore as they set out for a leasurely cruise.

"By the way Arthur, you won't need to cast another line for the remainder of the tournament."

"Why? I was just getting the hang of this and beginning to truly enjoy myself."

"Your magnificent marlin weighed in at 1001 lbs, a new record for these waters."

"No?"

"Si, the Cabans they haven't seen a fish like that since nineteen sixty nine."

"You don't say?"

"Why don't you relax aft and we'll find an empty stretch of sand up the coastline? The pink champagne's on ice, this one's on me!"

"Splendid. You know I've been thinking, 'La Perla' might not be such a bad idea, Cali."

"Oh Arthur."

"I knew you'd come around eventually."

"Yes, I have too much to lose, including my leading lady" as he reached out trying to grab the feisty female. His sombrero hit her in the forehead. She fell back and hit her head on the gunwale's hand rail. Arthur tried to revive her but lost his balance, He slipped off the side. As a last resort he gripped the rail tightly with his free hand, frantically trying to climb back onto the narrow gunwale. He looked like a floundering fool, his heavy cast waving wildly at his side. It only added to the force of gravity pulling him toward the restless surface of the water. In one last ditch effort he flung his arm up but caught Cali on the side of the head as she leaned forward to try and pull him up. She passed out and plummeted onto Arthur's sombrero. The tremendous added weight was too much for the tiring lunatic. He simply gave Cali a big bear hug as they hit the surface simultaneously. The sombrerro's string tightened around his neck as the straw parachute resisted the plunge. It slowed their gradual descent to the bottom near 'La Punta' the pinnacle at land's end. 'Divorce beach' up ahead to starboard as the craft continued to ride the waves oblivious to the lover's leap. The two entangled diver's embraced in each other's arms sank into the crystalline blue waters. Surprisingly, none of the other boats had noticed their dive. The couple came to rest among a shipwreck in 80' of water.

Pepe gave two blasts to signal an oncoming cruiser in the distance to veer right or starboard. He cranked the wheel in the same manner turning toward 'Divorce beach'. He waved his captain's hat. In the confusion and as a last resort, Dr Gum yelled "Stop the boat!" to the rest of the crew of the 'Treasure Chest'.

"I can't let that pirate win this competition!" he fumed. "I just can't come back empty handed."

"Well it's a long shot" insisted the seasoned anglers. "It has been known to occur but rarely that a couple of mighty big marlin have been hauled out near land's end."

"Wait, there's something on the sonar."

"What is it Garcia?"

"I don't know..... It's in the vicinity of that old shipwreck, I wouldn't give it the time of day!"

"Well time is of the essence! We've been out there all day and haven't caught a darn thing." Before you could say lickety split Dr Gum heaved his rod with a mighty motion of his arm. The line unreeled in a spinning whirring rush. "Here goes nothing."

Cali came around. The salty water stung her eyes. She screamed and expelled several bursts of precious oxygen at the sight of Arthur's bulging eyeballs looking back at her, ogling her in a garish ominous stare. They had been under for nearly three minutes. The sombrero string had sealed Arthur's fate in this watery grave. Her childhood diving days had acclimatized her for these descents. Hopefully all the wear and tear from her troubled teens, the extensive drug testing had not completely squashed her tremendous tidal volume. Cali's head and lungs ached as she fought feverishly to free herself from Arthur's bear hug. To com-pound the problem, they seemed to be snared among the seaweed and rusty rail of the wreck. In the few fleeting seconds her life flashed before her eyes. Such a shamble she thought, such a sordid mess. You ultimately reap what you sow she surmised as her head grew heavy and her sights grew dim. A sense of peace and tranquility over came her.

The Mexican crew came over to assist Dr Gum. Try as they might they could not free the hook.

"It must've caught part of the sunken wreck…"

"Or perhaps we've caught a really big one" yelled Dr Gum as he continued to yank on the line. He fell backward as several feet of line suddenly snapped back, then hooked onto something else. The resistance returned.

"You've caught something valuable from Davy Jone's locker" they joked.

"Enough to win the tournament?"

"We'll see." The crew failed to heave the heavy object out of the water.

"Give it one more tug, if you can't reel it in, Jose, you'll have to slip into your diving gear and cut the line. I hate to waste a good line for nothing!"

"Si."

Suddenly, the slippery specimen rose to the surface. Dr Gum had won the fierce contested battle. Cali was released from a similar fate as

Arthur as she sailed to the surface, leaving a bloody red trail in the clear blue water. It rapidly dissipated in the current.

"Still has some fight left in it!" he yelled. The pain in her arm was unbearable. She fought to free herself, fearing more for what awaited her at the surface. The haunting memory of her childhood 'catch and release' strengthened her resolve. In the struggle she tore a chunk of flesh from her forearm only to have her arm nearly ripped from it's socket as the hook caught the curvature of her ear and tore it off. Her body bobbed to the surface as Dr Gum flung the curled nacho shell or conch onto the deck. A red film like an aura enveloped the remains of Cali's cartilaginous ear.

"Good God!" he yelled. "It's a human ear!"

"I presume that's the rest of her."

"Shark attack?"

"Don't know! Come on, let's haul the body onboard!"

Cali squirmed like a crazed squid. Her arms flailing clawing until she came to. She realized she was afloat, somewhere out at sea. Her thoughts turned to an imminent shark attack as she felt the warm liquid ooze from her severed auricular appendage. A red slick slowly surrounded her head.

“Santa Maria!” shouted the startled fishermen. “Senorita, garb hold!” they yelled as they tossed her a life buoy.

**

Stacy fumbled with the keys to the shiny new souped up Mercedes. She had offered Consuela and two of the other staff from the Cabo Wabo to join her for an afternoon thrill ride up the coast. The staff stated that the ‘Hotel California’ was rumored to reside about 40 miles north. Stacy revved up the engine and inadvertently slammed it into reverse. The bright Porsche red Mercedes sailed off the dock and descended into the marina.

A fisherman tending his nets, tanked on tequila shook his head as the car descended below the surface in the neighboring stall.

“Yup, she got the Mercedes bends.”

23: Hotel California: Take 2

"They livin' it up at the Hotel California,
such a lovely place, such a lovely face"
- Don Henley, lyrics from
best selling album

The crew stood by Cali's side as she came to, lying in a bloody pool on the salty deck. Dr Gum applied pressure, dressed and draped the wound as best he could with his Bisbee's T-shirt. The captain gunned the engines roaring into the harbor. The coast guard in hot pursuit intent on apprehending the reckless speeder.

"Hurry!" the captain shouted as he slammed into the tires aside the breaker wall.

“Let’s get her to St Luke’s stat! shouted Dr Gum. The coast guard pinned the vessel to the water’s edge if they attempted to escape.

“It’s alright amigos, we have an emergency” Call IMSS, we’ll be there in a few minutes” insisted the astute Mexican captain.

The coast guard crew caught on to the unfurling dilemma immediately and boarded the ‘Treasure Chest’. The spirited professionals sprung into action immediately and carried Cali onto the dock. A Jeep Laredo had taken Arthur’s stall, where the shiny red roadster had once stood.

Cali awoke with a bandage woven tightly around her head. Dr Gum leaned over to the bewildered woman, the daugh-ter of Vincent van Gogh? She displayed the same self destructive tendencies. The tox screen had found elevated levels of cocaine and several other residual elements in her systemic circulation. A flash of déjà vu struck her.

“I’ve been her before” she stated groggily.

“Sorry miss, you’re confused, you’ve never checked into St Luke’s before!” said the astute nurses monitoring her vitals from the PC tablet.

“No, I mean…..I recognize your face” said

Cali as she studied Dr Gum's features.

"You must have me mistaken for someone else. It's probably the morphine I apologize for the gash on your arm. I'm not the greatest fisherman."

She held her stitched and bandaged arm tenderly then raised her fingers to her face and turban. "Yes, I remember. You saved my life before."

"I really don't recall.."

"You saved my life from the rabid anglers. They threw me back. My face, you saved my life!"

"Cali? Could it be? After all these years? I can't be!"

"Yes, our paths were destined to cross again, I felt it when we shook hands the other night. Our life lines touched."

"That's bizarre, but I do vaguely remember a young child who was brought in off one of the Channel Islands, Dr Chin did most of the dirty work reconstructing your beautiful face. My how you've matured."

"More than you'll ever know."

"You've blossomed into such a stunningly beautiful woman. There wasn't a day that went by that I didn't wonder what had become of you. You vanished without a trace. You were an aspiring actress weren't you? I often saw ghostly reminders of you on the billboards, but the name was altered."

"My life took a turn for the worst. I gradually descended into my own person -al hell. The drugs, the one night stands. It wasn't until I met Dr Arthur that I thought they'd finally turn around. By the way I assume you found his body."

"What do you mean?"

"Let's let her rest, she's confused." "The body! Arthur jumped ship or fell overboard I don't remember. He was dangling from the side of the gunwale rail hanging on for his dear life."

"No, no one mentioned…"

"I reached over to try and pull him up. The last thing I remember I caught a surprise left hook from his cast."

"That's preposterous, I told him to stay away from the water. I put the cast on his arm myself just yesterday afternoon."

"I know it all sounds so crazy, but you've got to believe me!"

"Alright we'll check it out."

"Now get some rest, you've been through one hell of an ordeal."

"And the 'Dreamweaver', why didn't they come back for us?"

"You must be dreaming" rationalized the skeptical senorita.

"No, she's telling the truth, I do recall even meeting the captain, Pepe" defended said Dr Gum.

"We get all kinds in here, mostly the converted 'teetolers', tanked on teq-uila, destined for detox. We've heard it all. All sorts of sordid fish stories..."

"Thanks, you've been very helpful" said Dr Gum cutting her off.

Dr Gum returned to the marina. A large water laiden rock lobster red Mercedes was fished out of the harbor. The seaweed dangled from the doors, chrome trim and spoked wheels.

"Wasn't that Arthur's?"

"She must've got the Mercedes Bends" laughed the police chief. The four shivering passengers had narrowly escaped with their lives.

"Where's Arthur? Isn't he back?"

“No, he hasn’t returned. Did anyone else see him leave on the ‘Dreamweaver?”

“No boat ever registered by that name” said the Mexican chief flipping his port of call registry.

“Something smells fishy here.”

“I need a shower” said one of the staff members, I can’t go back to work smelling like a fish hatchery.”

“Is Cali the only one on top of things? Can’t you at least check up on her claim?”

“Sure, doc, later.”

**

The harbor patrol found the mutilated remains of Arthur. The soggy sombrero still strapped to his head. In the short time at the bottom, several species had already begun to feast on him, fresh fish meal as far as they were concerned.

The report was a long time comin’.

“It appears Arthur embezzled the HCFC out of millions, took the staff pensions…..Take the money and run I always say. The ‘Dream weaver’ ran aground on the shore of an uncharted isle up the coast, engine trouble they figured.

The vast heap of salt of Cedros Island, as

hospitable as the salt mines of Siberia. Some of the girls were carved up bad.

The crew must have resorted to cannibalism, they all eventually starved to death."

"That's it?"

"I have heard several conflicting stories" said Sperry Sr. who flew in immediately to San Jose Int'l.

"My son will receive a full funeral service inspite of his misadventure. I've arranged to have him set to rest in Colmar, near the founder of the Bank of America and William Randolph Hearst, some of my forefather's colleagues. I don't know if he actually embezzled me out of billions? Per - sonally, he fell in with the wrong crowd. The thousands of staff pension funds are gone! Bob Maxwell's attempted suicide or heart attack as he plunged off the 'Lady Ghislaine', too faced billions in debt. Perhaps the drug king pins milked us? Then redistributed the vast fortune to their baby cartels, in this never ending battle against evil. I told him to stay north of the border. Oh by the way, the American Inmarsat satellite and Baja ground crew confirmed the buggy stolen in La Paz was

Arthur's. They began to worry when the 'Lone Ranger' lagged behind the pack back to Ensenada. Apparently Arthur had informed the pit crew he was heading here to Cabos. Who could have foreseen that his fate would be sealed at land's end of all places? He had such a promising career ahead of him, both as a physician and aspiring film producer."

"I guess he was true to his heart and followed his dream" said Dr Gum solemnly. "He'll be sadly dearly missed by all of his colleagues."

"Thank you."

"Oh, you and your clumsy buffoons here in Baja have some serious explaining to do" snapped Sperry Sr.

"And how is that?"

"The girls were butchered, just like the bodies they found in 'la Bahia de muertos' near La Paz."

"The bay of the dead? My trusty Mexican crew had mentioned strange midnight sightings. Fisherman simply leaving their bait, and not reaping what they sowed."

"It turned out that the call girls in the region were not returning their calls. Their phones off the hook so to speak. These so called 'fishermen' were actually part of a highly sophisticated cartel net-work. The girls were in transit awaiting transport to foreign ports. Their augmented pass-ports, the breast implants were priceless. The means to support the crafty trade. They were reduced to mules alive, then in the end fish meal and bait. Those that made it this far."

"You mean they were carriers?"

"Yes, a continuous stream of cocaine. They were ultimately bound for exclusive clinics in southern California for the reduction mammoplasty procedures."

"A deadly double dose of trouble."

"So the girl I tried to save at the 'Hotel California' had succumbed to a toxic cocaine overdose, as one or both of her implants burst?" asked Cali.

"We may never know unless we exhume the body."

"Let here rest in peace, along with the others in La Paz. God only knows how many poor souls are out there waiting to die or will succumb to their ruthless slaughter and go under the knife just to escape a fate worse than death."

"It looks like you made it!" said Dr Gum.

"Everyone deserves a second chance

"If it weren't for you…." she began to cry.

"Lightning does strike twice."

**

Dr Gum and Cali spent a beautiful candle lit dinner in a castle high atop the 'enchanted hill' in San Simeon.

"It's the perfect fairy tale ending to our miraculous reacquaintance" commented Cali peering out into the pacific. They sat on one of the numerous terraces of magnificent 90,000 sq. ft structure, a compilation of some of the most outstanding architectural treasures of it's day. The former residence of America's 1st media movie mogul W.R. Hearst, an icon, an inspiration. The 200 + film and cartoon collection classics, including the first syndication left by the legendary producer are still enjoyed by all. Citizen Kane, a sketch of William Randolph Hearst and other prominent men at the time is ranked # 1 of the American Film Institute's 100 greatest films of all time. Perhaps a remake is in the air?" asked Dr

Gum.

"One has to dream big!" insisted Cali. They were up early enjoying a beautiful California sunrise, then set out on the road again.

"I have a little surprise for you Cali, close your eyes" said Dr Gum as they cruised along the Pacific Coast highway toward Ventura.

"Remember what I said about second chances? No peeking."

"Yes" They pulled into the parking lot of the quaint CSUCI campus. California State University Channel Islands. She screamed as she saw her former accomodations.

"What's the matter?"

"Is this your sick idea of surprise, you're joking aren't you? I'll never go back to that asylum."

"Asylum? Camarillo closed it's doors in 1997. They reopened in 2002, CSUCI is the new California state run university, one of the best. I thought I'd kick start your career. Brush up on your academia and acting lessons."

"I can't believe it" she cried.

"A lot of famous performers passed through these halls, most of them returned to continue their successful careers. There's no reason you can't accomplish the same success!"

"Thank you" she hugged him.

"You can check in next month it's only a four year program. You can come to the big city, anytime to audition for a really big role. I told a few of my patients, including some noted producers, about you. They'd love to see you, and have arranged for you to stay at the pink palace, the Beverly Hills Hotel. It's a beautiful room looking into the exquisite courtyard garden."

"You mean the hotel on the cover of the Eagle's album?"

"The 'Hotel California', the real McCoy, the one and only. They felt you've earned it."

"You're too much."

"Oh, I've planned another little surprise. The Cadillac pulled off the freeway into the ferry landing in Huntington beach, for a short hop to Avalon, where she spent her first formative years. A much happier time free from all the curve balls life had thrown her.

They paid their respects to another great man, by placing a wreath at the William Wrigley memorial botanical garden.

Cali reflected on her short action packed life, all the colorful characters she had met along the convoluted route, the crazy road trips, close encounters, the brushes with certain death, full of adventures. She wondered what had become of the 'Cadillac Crooners', probably buried the pink Cadillac with all the others in Amarillo, Texas, America's Stonehenge.

"And to top it off …" A California National Park service ranger slowly stepped out from behind the memorial.

"My you've grown" he said with a tear in his eye. "You probably won't remember me, but I held you in my arms so many years ago."

"How could I forget?" she said as she ran to give him a big bear hug. She recognized the bear on his Golden State hat right away. "I want you to have some-thing." Another park ranger brought out a small eagle clinging to his forearm.

"I can't keep her, she deserves to make it on her own hook. Let her go, she's a free bird."

The ranger raised his arm, the bird took to flight, soaring above the memorial.

"We've set about 43 golden eagles free over the past couple of years. We knew they'd eventually learn to fly. It took a little coaching though.

EPILOGUE

A strange convoluted fish story indeed. The life lines of three people woven in a web of dramatic twists, deceit and deadly consequences. The very wealthy, able to squander fortunes, as the saying goes 'a fool and his money are soon parted.' The middle of the road, the slow and steady turtles, who earn it by their own hook, then the tortured victims at the bottom of life's barrel, squashed and stymied in the process. So many more innocent lives were drawn into the net, effected whether they liked it or not. The deadly cartels continue their export business finding ever more elusive ways to evade the concerted efforts of the combined forces of the DEA, the drug and crime units of law enforcement. Their level of sophistication seeming to outpace the positive progress made. Precious resources are wasted on people who return to guide the cartels in their mission to bring the cash crops to the United States, where they decimate the minds of America's youth. Hooked only temporarily, lost but found again, hope (esperanza), ultimately restored.

BIBLIOGRAPHY

Catch the Big One? Hooked on Bisbee's www.bisbees.com world's richest blue-fish tournament Cabos San Lucas, Baja

America's cup adventure, San Diego 1995
32nd www.americascup.com Spain 2007

Hotel California 1) Beverley Hills Hotel, cover of Eagles album.
2) Camarllo State hospital closed '97
now CSUCI www.csuci.edu
3) Todos, Mexico? Facsimile?

Caliburn: King Arthur's Sword

California history and mixed bag of facts

W.R. Hearst, movie media mogul's castle
San Simeon, CA www.hearstcastle.com

Del Coronado Hotel, www.hoteldel.com
San Diego, CA

Cabos San Lucas festivities, Cabo Wabo, Giggling Marlin, Squid Row

Author's Cosmetic Bondodontist Conf. 1995, Cabos San Lucas, Mexico

The author, Bernie Unrau, a dentist by training, stumbled across a four minute video back in 1989, an interview with the prolific Robin Cook, a physician by training. His mastery of the medical thriller inspired Bernie to embark on a 2nd career and a new uncharted course. The central character in his novels, Dr Gum, perhaps part bumbling lieutenant Columbo or the deductive Sherlock Holmes the imaginary detective created by Sir Conan Doyle, also a physician; the tenacity of Dr

Ryan conceived by Tom Clancy, or the curiosity of Indiana Jones A dash of the dapper James Bond blended in, shaken and stirred into the equation the inspiration of in depth concept research of Michael Crichton and his creations or the powerful suspense of a John Grisham legalistic thriller. Or to simply bring some of his years as a dentist, lecturer and inventor to light by engaging in espionage, elucidating an enigma, disclosing the dastardly or diabolical scheme, or dreaming up a formidable frightening future. And as the prolific Zane Grey, dentist turned novelist turned screenwriter at the turn of the century, pen 100 books. The author has enjoyed travel, tennis, sailing, skiing, flying, reading and thinking. He is single and currently resides in Calgary, Alberta.

Books by Dr Bernie Unrau:

Terra Vista
Deadly Implant
Not A Drop
Golden Mask
Questa
Rook
Hooked
Big B
Enlightened
The Board
The ROM
New Millenium
Reflections
Submarine Slide
Sabotage
Dentinator
Ubar
Stemwinder
Pulling Strings
Meltdown
Pulpit Fiction
Confusion
Glazers
God Almighty
The Scrying
Rising
Cravings
Fantastic Voyage III
East of Aden
The X Files: The Grey Zone
Lacryma Christi
In Gold We Trust
Lion Island
Dead Hand

Dream Big
The Fifth Pillar

Screenplays by Dr Bernie Unrau:

Terra Vista
Deadly Implant
Not A Drop
Golden Mask
Questa
Rook
Hooked
Big B
Enlightened
The Board
The ROM
New Millenium
Reflections
Submarine Slide
Sabotage
Dentinator
Ubar
Stemwinder
Pulling Strings
Meltdown
Pulpit Fiction
Confusion
Glazers
God Almighty
The Scrying
Rising
Fantastic Voyage III
East of Aden
Cravings
The X Files: the Grey Zone
Chokepoint

Ultra Stealth: War Game
Phantom of the Operatory
Montauk Monster
Deep Fright
Jabberwhacky
Pandemonium
Deep Fright: Down Under
The Curse of the 7 Pagodas
Sweet Tooth
The Ice Forest
The Frozen Chosen
Insight
Subterranea
The Glass
Deep Fright: Deep Freeze
Sky Parlor
The Movie Mobile
Nightwalker
Venus' Grotto
Big Fat Liar 2
The Space Bar
Spearphish
Mind At Large
Summa Gate
Not Yet
Finger of God
Terror Island
Game Over
Salt II
Death Valley Riders
Apes & Aliens
Zombie Street
Catch Me When You Can
Bloody Mary
Raid
Bury Me Under The Volcano

The Privateers
Bond Jane Bond
You Can't Take It With You
Catch 22
The Float House
Alien Vengeance
Alien Vengeance: Raising Cain
The Great Museum Heist
Magic is in the Hare
Goldfield
Quicksilver
Bad to the Bone
In Gold We Trust
Lion Island
Dead Hand
The Fifth Pillar

Made in the USA
Las Vegas, NV
21 September 2026

54953730R00187